W9-BLR-948

STICKLEBACKS
and
SNOW GLOBES

STICKLEBACKS
and
SNOW GLOBES

B.A. GOODJOHN

THE PERMANENT PRESS
Sag Harbor, NY 11963

For information, address:
The Permanent Press
4170 Noyac Road
Sag Harbor, NY 11963
www.thepermanentpress.com

Library of Congress Cataloging-in-Publication Data

Goodjohn, B.A.
    Sticklebacks and snow globes / B.A. Goodjohn.
        p. cm.

    ISBN-13: 978-1-57962-155-1 (alk. paper)
    ISBN-10: 1-57962-155-4 (alk. paper)

    1. Girls—Fiction. 2. Epileptic children—Fiction. 3. London (England)—Fiction. I. Title.

PS3607.O5636S75 2007
813'.6—dc22   2007025373

Printed in the United States of America.

Contents

For Jim Peterson and Kay Sexton.
Their honesty and friendship touches my heart and
each page of this book.

WINTER 1971

There was a unicorn in my first snow globe. It had "With Luck from Ramsgate" in gold letters on the base. I haven't got it anymore. Dorothy let all the water out.

I've still got twelve. Seven up there on my windowsill, and five on that shelf over my bed. That's where I put my favourites. I'm going to give "Jesus in the Wilderness" to my sister though. It's got yellow snow.

My sister says snow globes are just things in glass balls, but she's wrong. It's like the whole world's inside, ready to shake. You can fit anything in there. Little things like squirrels. Or big things like the Taj Mahal. That's in India where Keesal comes from.

Before you shake one, everything's quiet. All the flakes lie on the flat bits of the special thing inside—like in this reindeer one. See? In between his antlers. On his hooves. It's Christmas in there forever.

You can wish on snow globes. You could pick up Blenheim Palace, shut your eyes and shout ROOF! Then shake. If snow falls on the turrets, like you said, your wish comes true. But it has to be sitting in a thick layer right over the pink tiles. Thick enough for you to dig your nail in. If you could.

It doesn't count if you shake it again.

Dad's going to put Dizzy in one. He's going to fit all of New Orleans in there.

The Ghost Note

"There is a technique called the ghost note. It involves using the tongue to arrest airflow just as a note is begun. By pressing the tongue against the mouthpiece, the note sounds as if it has disappeared. That the note has been is never in doubt. But it disappears as magically as a dove from a linen handkerchief."

—J.T. PARKER

Donald Thompson, toasty in red long johns and undershirt, laid his freshly laundered overalls across the ottoman and took his trumpet from its open case on the bed. He pressed his tongue against the brass mouthpiece—he loved the feel of the smooth metal in his mouth—and ran the tips of his fingers across its stone-inlaid buttons, not pressing, merely gauging the coolness of the Brazilian Agate.

"Dizzy had these," he said to the fat man in the cheval glass. "Dizzy had these and played notes so sweet they sugared people's hearts." He inhaled, blew a note, then tried to stop it with his tongue. It was almost a ghost note, a note that was never there. He filled his lungs and played the opening bars to "Nobody Knows," then put the trumpet on the bed, the brass valves disappearing through the looped holes in the crocheted bed cover. He pulled out a creased airmail letter from the case and read it. A snort from the wardrobe interrupted his concentration. He put down the letter and pulled open the wardrobe door. Inside sat his daughter.

"Sweet Thing!" he said. "What are you doing in there?"

Eight-year-old Tot Thompson was partly obscured by the hems of her mother's dresses, her small red T-bar shoes flanked

by high-heeled court shoes and ink-spattered work boots. She
was a small, thin child, her hair a strange mass of orange curls
that kinked straight out from her head like a clown's wig. Her
eyes were shut tight, and her pale hands quivered in the air as if
playing an invisible piano.

He smiled and picked up the trumpet again.

"Ladies and gentlemen, tonight we have Donald Thompson
on the trumpet, accompanied by . . . " he gestured to the wardrobe, "the one, the only, Steeeeevie Wonder!" He put the
trumpet to his lips and picked up where he had left off, the sad
strains of the blues classic once again filling the room. The trees
through the window waved their bare branches in sympathy
with the music's heartbreak, and a drift of swallows swooped
in and around the Ccommunity Centre eaves. Reflected in
the mirror, he could see Tot's hands reaching out beyond the
wardrobe door, fluttering in the air. All is good in the world,
he thought. Just me, the birds, and the sweetest little air piano
player to come off the Bishop's Croft housing estate.

His wife appeared carrying an armload of laundry.

"You're going to be late," she said. "Are you going to put
those overalls on or what?" She dropped the clothes on the
bed. He turned and watched her sort underwear into "his" and
"her" piles.

"I've still got five minutes," he said, shining the trumpet's
bell on the hem of his shirt. "I thought I'd walk Tot to school
on my way in."

"I wish I had a minute to spare!" She reached for her own
pile of underwear, each piece a froth of cheap lace and satin
ribbon. "Seems everyone's got time around here. Apart from me,
that is." He watched her expertly manoeuvre the wardrobe door
fully open with her knee, her arms laden with laundry. Tot still
sat playing piano among the shoes, but now a puddle of urine
collected around the heels of his wife's shiny court shoes.

"For God's sake, Donald!" Elaine shouted. "She's had
another bloody fit!" She scooped up the child. "Can't you be
trusted to even look after your own daughter?" She rushed out
of the room towards the bathroom, leaving a shower of panties

and camisoles on the floor behind her. He turned back to the cheval glass, his trumpet hanging from his hand, and shook his head at the man in the mirror.

"I thought she was doing Stevie," he said. "Elaine!" he shouted down the hall, "I thought she was doing Stevie!"

There was no answer from the bathroom, just the drum of water against the basin.

He put the trumpet on the ottoman and stepped into the blue twill overalls. He eased the fabric past the bulk of his stomach and pulled the buttons across to the buttonholes. His fingertips caught on the rough fabric, each tip stained navy from years of mixing ink for the newspaper company across town. Something caught his eye. Tot's rabbit hopped from the open wardrobe and headed out across the lilac shag-pile carpet. He tried to grab the animal, but it was too quick. All that was left was a cluster of droppings nestled on a pair of his wife's lacy knickers.

* * * * *

Donald opened the leather trumpet case and slid it onto the padded seat next to him. He drained the last of his whiskey, spinning the ice around in the empty glass. He thought the lunchtime session had gone well. The Blue Notes—himself on trumpet, Ken on drums, Jimmy on sax and Carol, the queen of vocals—had given a good set, starting out with their old favourites, then finishing up with a medley of ragtime classics.

In the back room, Ken was sorting out the wages with the landlord, and Carol and Jimmy sat at the bar chatting with the barmaid. Jimmy's straw hat lay discarded on the bench by the dartboard. He'd have to have a word with him about that while Ken divvied up the money. After all, the punters came to see traditional jazz and expected to see the boys in boaters and striped blazers.

He watched Carol, the latest member of The Blue Notes. She had her back to him and wore a black sheath dress with a long electric-blue feather in her hair. She always dressed too exotically for the lunchtime slot. When he'd mentioned it to her, she'd shaken her head at him, her blonde hair a mass of plump curls. "I'm not like you lot. I'm going to make it big," she'd told him. "You never know who's sitting out there in the crowd, Donnie. You've got to be ready to make your move."

At her interview last month in his dining room, she told him she wanted fame before she was thirty, to leave England, maybe tour Vegas with a band. His wife, who had been making the tea and eavesdropping, told him that if Carol was in her twenties, she'd lived a hard life. But whatever her age, her voice was something else.

Sometimes, when her voice and his trumpet hit the notes just right, he felt his stomach quiver. It reminded him of the feeling he used to get as a kid swinging on tyres over the river, of that moment when the rope reaches its longest stretch and the tyre hangs in the air, in the second before it rushes back down towards the water. Her voice and his trumpet could take him there. For a moment, he would be held against a memory of water and sky. Those stretched seconds seemed almost mystical, as if there was something or someone else in the room, something blameless and full of light.

He never told her because it wasn't really about Carol. It wasn't even about him. It was about her hitting the note and his trumpet bedding down beneath it. There was no other word for it. It was magical.

He unscrewed the mouthpiece and put it away in its leather pouch, then eased the trumpet back into its case, the worn mauve velvet caressing the glow of the brass valves and bell. The set was over and another week of family and factory was about to begin as it had begun so many times before.

Donald and Elaine had moved to Stanley Close in '65. After their second daughter, Tot, was born, the two-bedroom flat in Harlow wasn't big enough, and Elaine managed to arrange a council swap onto the Bishop's Croft housing estate. Tot was perhaps a year old and Dorothy about seven. Elaine spent that first year coping with stretch marks and colour swatches. She'd refused the free wallpaper offered to tenants by the local council. Said she couldn't live surrounded by Nova-mura Bamboo and Chinese Temples. Then she made him rip out the old kitchen cabinets and replace them with solid-wood units from John Lewis. He told her the council would have their arses in a sling if they found out, but he'd done it anyway.

The last six years had been hard. The women in the road disliked Elaine. They reckoned she was stuck-up, and the men despised him for the pushover he'd become. Their attitude didn't bother Elaine. She told him if the residents of Stanley Close had taken them to their hearts, it would have been proof the Thompsons were doing something wrong. And after all, she'd pointed out, it wasn't as if they would be staying on the estate long, would they?

Still, over the years, he had often wished he fitted in more. It would have been nice to have a chat with the other Stanley Close men over a beer, maybe join in with the general bitching about wives and football. But it never happened. The neighbours smiled and nodded as they trimmed their hedges or mowed their lawns, but they never actually spoke to him. Apart from being on first-name terms with the Deepens family—mainly due to Jimmy's role as sax player in The Blue Notes—Elaine and her primping and preening had put them outside the group. He didn't really mind any more. Not after he hatched his plan.

He watched Jimmy finish his beer and drop his sax into a plastic carrier bag. On the walk home, he'd tell him about the letter from America. He'd have a bit of a laugh with him first. Pull his leg about the straw boater and tell him how they all wear them on Bourbon Street. He sipped his whiskey, antici-pating the moment when he'd tell young Jimmy about the deal he'd struck.

The bar emptied as the locals finally finished their drinks and went home. Carol still chatted to the barmaid, and Ken was nowhere to be seen. He was polishing his open trumpet case with his handkerchief when someone tapped him on the shoulder. It was Jimmy.

"No easy way to say this, Don," Jimmy mumbled, passing the bag with the sax from one hand to another, "but I'm giving it up."

Donald clicked shut the lid of the case. "Giving what up, Jim?" he said, smiling. "The beer? Cathy got you to sign the pledge?"

"No," said Jimmy, looking down at the floor. "The band. I've had enough of this Sunday lark. I'm getting rid of the sax. Swapping it."

"Swapping it?" he asked. "What the hell for?"

"A set of clubs. Me and the wife are taking up golf. She's fed up with me being out all the time, what with practicing and being up here every Sunday. And now with the promotion, it seems, well . . . Cathy reckons it would be a good career move."

Donald shook his head as if seawater flooded his ears. "You can't let them do this to you, Jim," he said. "Let *her* take up golf. Take the kids pony riding in the Brecon bloody Beacons. Anything. But don't let her make you give up playing. It's . . . it's everything."

Jimmy sat down on the bench opposite and drew patterns in the spilt beer pooling on the tabletop. "No, not for me, it's not, Don. I agree with her." He looked hard at Donald. "It's time for me to move up."

"But music's our way up. How many nights have we talked about it, Jim? New Orleans? Bourbon Street? The whole thing. You and me. We've talked about it."

Jim stood and picked up the carrier bag. "That was just beer talking, Don. Just the beer. We ain't ever leaving here. You'll be playing 'Stranger on the Shore' until you die. 'The Blue Notes at The Eagle.' That's it. That's all there is." He fiddled with his empty beer glass, turning it between his thumb and middle finger.

"But, Jimmy," Donald said, flipping open his case and pulling out the letter, "It's happened! The U.S. of A! We're out of here!"

"Never a truer word said, mate," Jimmy replied, setting down his glass on the table and pulling on his jacket. "I'm gone. I'm late for my dinner."

"Read it, for Christ's sake!" Donald slapped the letter on the table and pushed it towards Jimmy. "I'm talking America, and you're talking about your stomach?"

Jimmy flicked the letter back across the table. It came to a halt in a small puddle of beer. "No, I'm talking reality, Don. I've got a good job, a son, and another kiddie on the way. You're talking pipe dreams." He drained his pint. "Now, I'm off. Tell Ken I'll pick up my money in the week. I'll do next Sunday, but that's it. Weather permitting, me and Cathy'll be playing golf now on Sundays. Who knows? We may even join the country club!" Jimmy held out his hand. "No hard feelings, Don," he said. Donald sat there, shaking his head. Jimmy shrugged and walked out, his bag bumping against the pub door with a tinny thud.

Donald put the letter in his pocket and shut the trumpet case. He thought about what Jimmy had said about America being a pipe dream, about it just being the drink talking. He thought about his family, about Tot playing football in the back garden. She took after him, practiced for hours and hours. She was the centre forward, the goalie, the crowd; he shut his eyes and could see his eldest running through the piano scales, her tongue clamped between her lips; Elaine in the kitchen, watching some *haute-cuisine* cookery program on the portable black and white.

He studied Carol at the bar, the beginnings of a potbelly straining at the slippery fabric of her dress. The feather in her hair had come unclipped and trailed across her bare shoulder. Ken reappeared from the manager's office and slipped onto a bar stool next to her. His hand snaked around her waist and massaged her shiny love handles.

Donald looked away. "They don't get it," he said to the empty glass. "It wasn't the drink talking. For me, it was never the drink."

* * * * *

He parked the car outside his house in the corner of Stanley Close and turned off the engine. It was raining and the neat beds of winter pansies that flanked the concrete pathway looked waterlogged and bruised. Next door, their new neighbour, Mr. Damson, a macintosh tented over his head, was putting a rake away in his potting shed. He waved and Donald nodded through the rain-beaded glass of the windscreen. He pulled the keys from the ignition, got out, and slammed the door. Mr. Damson disappeared down his alley, closing his back gate behind him.

He walked down the garden path, and before he could slip his key into the lock, the front door swung open and young Lilly O'Flannery, his eldest's best friend from number seven, rushed out onto the steps.

"Afternoon, Lilly," he said, straightening his blazer. "In a hurry?"

"Sorry, Mr. Thompson," she said. "It's my tea. I'm late for my tea." She turned and ran across the pavement and over the grass. He watched her go, her yellow hair streaming behind her, then went into the house and shut the door. In the hallway, he fingered the letter in his pocket, then quietly climbed the stairs.

Downstairs, he could hear his wife chopping vegetables and a discordant piano rendition of "Silent Night" from the dining room. As he sat down on the bed to reread the letter, something moved in the open wardrobe. He pulled back the door and found Tot sitting among the shoes, her rabbit on her lap.

"Are you alright?" he asked, placing his hand on her forehead, checking her temperature.

She nodded.

"I'm sorry about Friday," he said. "I didn't realise. I thought you were being Stevie. You know, playing."

She stroked the rabbit. The animal chewed on a long strip of carrot. It looked at him and scrunched its nose. Tot put the rabbit in the wire basket with her mother's underwear. "I don't mind being sick and taking tablets," she said, "but it's Barney." She looked at the rabbit behind the wire, rare tears collecting in her eyes.

"What's wrong with Barney?" he asked.

She stroked the animal's long black ears. "I'm frightened I might drop him again. You know, when the fit thing happens. And he might get a broken head. Or a leg. Or he might get away and get eaten by Uncle Ernie's dog. Or a fox."

He smoothed her wayward orange hair with his hand. She looked up at him. "I'm not frightened of Kit-the-Fit," she said. "I just don't want him to hurt Barney."

Donald picked up his trumpet case and took the rabbit from the wire basket. "Come on, Sweet Thing. I've got an idea." They walked out to the hall and into the bathroom, closing the door behind them.

He gently placed the rabbit in the bathtub and rested his trumpet case on the basin.

"Go on, jump in," he said.

Tot climbed into the bath and sat cross-legged at the plug end. The rabbit scrabbled about on the slippery porcelain surface, but despite several efforts, could not scale the sides.

"You see," he said. "If Kit-the-Fit comes calling now, you won't drop Barney, and he can't run away.

"But we can't stay in the bath forever."

"No, not for ever, Sweetie. But it's nice now and again, isn't it? Not having to worry?"

"Yeah," she agreed. "Can I have that towel?" She pointed at the rack on the wall behind him, and he passed her a fluffy green towel. She wound it round her head like a turban. "So I don't hurt my head if Kit comes back," she explained. "Now I don't have to worry about anything!" She smiled and played with the soap dish, filling it up with a handful of carrot strips from her skirt pocket.

"You know, Tot," he said, "that's all I want." He pulled a sheet of music from his trumpet case and stuck it to the mirror with a blob of toothpaste. "Can you keep a secret, a big secret?"

She nodded.

"You see," he said, not looking away from the music, removing the mouthpiece from its pouch, "Daddy might be going away. To New Orleans. I got this letter from your Uncle Trevor." He pulled out the envelope from his pocket. Barney lost his grip on the side of the tub and slid back down to the tap end, coming to a halt by Tot's knees and the soap dish. The rabbit chewed on a carrot strip, the pair of them watching Donald from the bathtub.

He screwed the mouthpiece gently into the receiver. "Your Uncle Trevor's bought another bistro. Not on Bourbon Street, but close by. But I need to make sure you'll all be all right. If I go, like."

Tot picked up Barney and placed him in the plastic tidy behind the taps. "Is N'orleans in America?"

"Yes, in the South. The Home of Jazz, they say. It's where Dizzy used to play. I've told you about Dizzy, right?"

Tot chewed on her lip for a moment, then nodded. "He was the man with the 'narmonies."

He smiled. "Trevor wants me to come in with him, you see. To expand. You know—get a licence, put on live music at the weekend. I mean, who knows where we could go?"

He turned back to the sheet music and played a pure note to the fat man in the bathroom mirror. "Dizzy was the first true bop trumpet player. He was the king of rhythm."

The rabbit nibbled on Elaine's natural sea sponge, brown fronds spilling out the sides of its mouth.

"I've got to go, Tot. It's an opportunity of a lifetime."

"Can we come?" Tot scratched the animal's ears.

He shook his head as the rabbit spat out a brown mass onto the tiled splash back.

"Will you bring me back a present?" she said, mopping up the mess with a cotton wool ball.

"I'll send you something. What would you like?"

"Another snow globe. N'orleans in the snow?"

Donald nodded. He put the trumpet to his lips and tears rolled slowly down his face, then trickled into the corners of his mouth. He inhaled, breath building in his lungs. He closed his eyes, slowly forced the air smoothly through the mouthpiece, then pressed his tongue against the brass opening. The ghost note filled the small, square bathroom, echoed off the clean, white-tiled walls, then disappeared before it had even begun.

Sometimes you can have too much.

Take marbles.

I've only got pee-wees—the ones that look like they've got twisty fish in the middle—and if someone plays me for keeps and I lose them all, I can buy some more when I get my pocket money. But if someone's got a bag of swanky agates, like from their grandma or something, and their best is a blue and red corkscrew, and even their worst one is a lemon oxblood, and they play me and I win them all, they've lost everything. It's . . . all . . . gone.

Never play marbles with Michael O'Flannery. He calls his ballbies, but they're really ball-bearings his dad brings home from the ink factory. They're okay with pee-wees, but they'll smash an oxblood to smither-bloody-reens.

Scouting

✤

Dorothy Thompson's mother had taught her many things. Small things like not wearing green eye shadow with blue mascara or dark tights with pale shoes. And some sit-down big things. The first sit-down big thing she learned was that a woman can't let opportunities slip through her fingers, no matter how wet her nail varnish might be.

When Dorothy graduated from the Bishop's Croft junior school to the grammar school in Treeverton two years earlier, she realised she had been handed a sit-down opportunity of beautiful magnitude.

Her problem had always been their address: 17 Stanley Close. The close, tucked at the back of the council estate between the municipal dump and the small parade of shops—a newsagent's, a baker's, a butcher's, and a greengrocer's—was named after Stanley Baldwin, the British Prime Minister from the 1920s. The next road was Disraeli Avenue, then Churchill Rise, Asquith Avenue, Peel Place. They went on and on. Centuries of Prime Ministers giving their names to the brick-built homes that made up the Bishop's Croft council housing estate; her address told everyone she was a lowly council house kid.

The move up to the grammar school some twelve miles and two towns away had meant a new start: new friends, new teachers, new bus . . . and the opportunity for a new address. Dorothy had chosen Kings Road. Kings Road was at the farthest end of the Bishop's Croft village. The large private houses wound in a loop behind the Saxon-built village church, out of sight of the village shops, and some two miles away from Dorothy's house on the nearby council estate. The Kings Road mock Tudor houses with their beams and leaded windows were home to fathers who drove Beamers, kids who went to the private school, and to mothers who held coffee mornings and arranged flowers for the church services each Sunday.

She seized the sit-down opportunity and told her new school friends she lived in Kings Road.

* * * * *

When the church spire came into view, Dorothy grabbed her beret from her satchel and rammed it on her head. It was raining outside and already dark. The girl in the window seat next to her, who had been leaning over the headrest laughing with the two boys behind, settled back down.

"Are you positively one hundred percent sure you can't come to Norfolk with us next weekend?" the girl asked.

Dorothy picked up her satchel and slung it across her shoulder. "No, my mum won't let me stay out overnight. Sorry, Jen."

"That's so sad. There's going to be riding, and Daddy's hired a band and everything. Your mum and dad are so mean!"

She nodded as the bus slowed on the approach to the church and imagined the horror of turning up at a Norfolk point-to-point weekend with no riding clothes and nothing posh to wear for dinner.

Jen continued. "And you can't even have anyone back to your house or anything."

"It's because of mum's accident. She's in a wheelchair. She doesn't like anyone to see her. I told you that."

"Yeah, I know. Still. God! That must have been awful."

"What?"

"Breaking your neck go-go dancing. Did she really tour with Tom Jones? With a silver cage and everything?"

"Yeah. We don't talk about it much." The bus came to a halt. "Bye, Jen. Bye everyone."

On the street, the church windows were already a blaze of saints, all trudging along the road to heaven, their angular frames picked out in blue and gold. She always felt a bit guilty about the lies when she stood in front of the village church. So she turned her back on the saints, stuffed her hands into the pockets of her purple school blazer and began the two-mile walk home.

Lilly O'Flannery told her the lies would mean she'd burn in hell, but that was because Lilly was a Roman Catholic. The Thompsons were Church of England, and lying wasn't a burning offence. And anyway, she liked to think of it as not exactly lying—more inventing a new reality. She told her Treeverton friends her father was a musician, and that her mother had been a dancer. Both stories were nearly true. Her father played trumpet in a pub every Sunday, and her mother once auditioned for "Pan's People." She didn't get in. She wasn't tall enough. Dorothy didn't tell her new friends about Tot. After all, an annoying sister with epilepsy was hardly something to brag about.

The lampposts stopped on the outskirts of the village. Light spilt from the porches and windows of the big houses on either side of the road. She wondered what it would feel like to have a really big flashy car to drive around in or to shop at the boutique next to the chippie, where the dresses cost more than ten pounds. She imagined having one of those expensive little yappy dogs, the kind you could carry around in your handbag.

A car rumbled up behind her. She turned as it sped up through a puddle, drenching her with dirty water that soaked through her socks and school skirt. The driver wolf-whistled.

"Shitty bastard!" she shouted. "Shitty bloody bastard!"

It seemed the village lights faded at the same point that the taillights disappeared, and she began running for home. The faster she ran, the more she hated the big houses.

* * * * *

Dorothy and Lilly walked up Willowswitch Lane towards the village. Lilly, who went to Our Lady of the Holy Cross, was the closest thing she had to a real friend, but the relationship was in a state of constant flux. The two teenage girls continually vied for the upper hand. Each succeeded briefly and was then toppled by the other. Lilly's strong suit was her familiarity with the messy world of life and death. She provided information that Dorothy had to pretend to already know. It was Lilly who explained that you didn't get pregnant if the boy pulled his willy out before he came, and that condoms were an abomination in the eyes of God. Lilly, who had touched a dead man's face in a funeral parlour, helped her father with his meat rabbits, clearing the mucus and grime from mouths of rejected newborns, hand-feeding them, and then eventually killing them with a sharp blow to their dumb little skulls, just behind their long soft ears.

But if Lilly knew all there was to know about the intricacies of life and death, Dorothy was Queen of Ladylike. She knew what cutlery to use and in what order. She was the oracle of good taste and looked after her nails with a mock-tortoiseshell manicure kit. Dorothy's long brown hair was always sleek, and at night she brushed it a hundred times, softly counting the strokes out loud in the darkness of her bedroom.

When Lilly had suggested they go to the village fête, Dorothy's answer was an immediate yes. She loved to watch people who had money. It was an opportunity to learn how to do it right, and if she was ever going to land a big sit-down well-off boyfriend and move off the estate, she needed all the lessons she could get.

She had dressed with extra care, choosing brown velvet bell-bottoms and a peach angora sweater her mother had just finished paying for from the Kay's catalogue. The fuzzy sweater clung to her, showing off her nearly woman's body with its hand-span waist and teaspoon breasts.

She studied her friend. Lilly wore a pair of flared Levis, a tatty scoop-neck top, and a Dr. Who scarf. Her hair was long and blonde, and she was pretty in a hard kind of way. She seemed to be part woman, part child. She was buxom, even a little chubby in her face and arms, but her hips were slim to the point of bony and her gangly legs belonged to a little girl. It was as if she were slowly growing into her grown-up body from the shoulders down.

Ahead of them, a huge Sainsbury's lorry swung round into the lane, mounting the path with its front wheels. Lilly jumped back, and the lorry screeched to a halt, its air brakes squealing and hissing. The grinning driver leaned out the cab.

"You all right, darling?" he asked, leering at Lilly. She carried on walking, tossing her hair and pretending not to hear.

He tried again. "Fancy coming for a little ride, sweetheart?"

Lilly slowly turned around. She kissed the palm of her hand and, instead of blowing the kiss, stuck her fingers up and gave him the vee sign. He laughed, waved through the open window and drove off down the lane. Lilly ran her hand through her hair, and Dorothy could see she was blushing and smiling, all at the same time.

"Lilly O'Flannery," she said, "you'll get a name for yourself encouraging dirty lorry drivers!"

Lilly smoothed down her jumper. "I don't encourage them. But it's nice, isn't it."

"What is?"

"You know. When a man thinks you're pretty. I mean I'm in love with Nigel and all that, but. . . ."

"But what?"

"Don't you ever wish they'd just stop the lorry and take you off to Wales or somewhere? That'd be so romantic." She chewed on a strand of her hair. "It would be in the papers and everything. Maybe even on the news."

"Of course it wouldn't be romantic," Dorothy said. "They're dirty bastards. My mum said so. And she said it's vulgar to even look at them."

"Oh, Dorothy. You can be. . . ."

"What?"

"Oh, forget it!"

"No, I won't forget it, Miss Sticky!"

Lilly grabbed her arm and shook it. "Don't you ever call me that!" she said, her face inches from Dorothy's.

"Well," she said, "it's what all the boys call you. It's just a name."

Lilly's lips compressed into a hard blue line. "You don't call me that!"

Dorothy didn't answer.

"Right?" Lilly gripped her arm tighter, her fingernails sharp through the thin wool of her sweater.

Dorothy had never seen her this angry before. "Okay! All right!" She wrenched her arm from Lilly's grip. "Keep your knickers on!"

Lilly stomped ahead and walked in front all the way to the village. By the time they reached André's, the hairdressers, Dorothy was bored to tears with the silence and the argument. She caught up with Lilly and drew out two ten-pence pieces from her pocket.

"Go on," she said. "Have it. I get buckets of pocket money."

"I get pocket money. Loads of it." Lilly took the coins anyway.

Dorothy shrugged and Lilly stayed silent, but they resumed walking side by side through the village, which was busy with Saturday morning shoppers and other villagers heading for the fête.

Outside the wrought iron gates to the church hall, a Boy Scout marched up and down like a soldier on parade. Over his green uniform, he wore a sandwich board announcing the event and each time he about-turned, he cried out, "Come to the fête!"

Lilly poked Dorothy in the arm and grinned. "That's your boyfriend, that is!"

"S'not!" said Dorothy, poking her back. "He's yours! He's the one you want to marry, he is!"

Lilly bumped her towards the boy with her hip, then caught hold of Dorothy's waist before she toppled over into him. "You want to kiss him, you do!" The two girls, their argument forgotten, giggled and barged their way past the blushing Boy Scout into the hall.

The long room was packed with people and smelt of floor polish and fancy perfume. A chipped Jesus hung from a cross on the far wall below a clock, which was three hours slow. The vicar sat at the piano on the stage and picked out a halting rendition of "Delilah," much to the amusement of the three ladies who gazed at him with a mixture of awe and blatant attraction.

Wallpaper pasting tables lined the walls from the doorway to the stage. They bowed under bric-a-brac, pies and preserves, knitted scarves and mitten sets, concrete door stops, Dundee cakes, tea urns, tombola, bran dips, and Win-a-Goldfish games. Small boys in Cub Scout uniforms darted in and out of the tables and up onto the stage, and everywhere there were ladies in beautiful dresses wearing rows of pearls and sparkly brooches. Dorothy watched the three women on the stage, each one simpering and smiling at the vicar. The vicar, debonair in his black cassock and grey bell-bottoms, had finished "Delilah" and was trying to sip a cup of tea. Threatened by a horde of Cubs whooping and hollering across the stage, he held the cup above his head so as not to have it knocked from his grasp. "Boys, boys!" he called after them, "a little respect for God's stage and these lovely ladies wouldn't go amiss!"

"Don't he speak la di da!" whispered Lilly. "Look at all those stupid dresses!"

Dorothy watched her friend in her secondhand top and worn-out jeans.

"Where are we going first?" Lilly asked.

"I want to go round on my own for a while," she said. "I'll meet you back here in a quarter of an hour." She walked off before Lilly could object.

She stopped in front of a stall selling bookmarks and lamp-shades decorated with pressed flowers and leaves. A large lady in a blue silk dress and straw hat sat on a folding chair behind the table. By her feet was a picnic basket in which a tiny Pomeranian snuffled and snored. She had seen baskets like this in films on the telly. They usually sat propped in the bottom of a boat on a river, while a man moved oars through the water and a lady, just like this one, dozed on a mountain of cushions, trailing her fingers through blossom-smothered water.

The dog growled and Dorothy backed away.

"Can I help you, dear?" the woman asked.

Dorothy picked up a bookmark covered in pressed poppies.

"That's five pence," the woman said. "Real poppies, you know. I picked them myself last year. In Dorset."

The woman looked like the kind who baked cakes when it wasn't even someone's birthday. Dorothy handed over a five-pence piece, and the woman placed the bookmark in a paper bag. "Are you a Girl Guide, dear?" she said, handing her the bag. Dorothy shook her head. "A wonderful organisation. And of course, there's all those lovely Venture Scouts to chase after!" The woman turned away to serve a man holding a lampshade covered with dried ferns and sealed with transparent sticky-back Fablon.

Dorothy put the bag in her pocket and looked around. A couple of tables down, towards Jesus on the cross, was the "Break-a-Plate" stall. Two Boy Scouts were replenishing the shelves with old plates and cups and dishes. They were skinny boys about her age and proud in full uniform, right down to the plastic woggle slides on their neckerchiefs. The third, a Venture Scout, stood a little apart in front of a bin brimming with wooden balls. He wore beige trousers and an open-necked shirt. He looked like the kind of boy who'd never be seen dead wearing a woggle, even in private. His hair was long enough to cover his collar and curled at the back. He had soft eyes and a mouth that seemed too wide for his face and yet perfect, both at the same time. He was talking to an old lady who wore a green raffia hat with a large spray of roses on its brim. She kept touching his shoulder and smiling a hideous, yellow false-teeth smile.

Dorothy pushed forward, knocking the old lady with her elbow. "How much are the balls?" she asked.

"Young lady!" fussed the woman, flicking her gloves at Dorothy. "Have you never heard of `excuse me'?"

"Here you are, Mrs. Spencer." The boy handed a pot of African violets to the elderly woman. "You win a prize for wearing the most attractive hat of the morning!"

The woman smiled, adjusted her hair, and pinched the handsome boy's cheek. "It's nice to see some young people with manners. They don't cost anything you know, missy!" She took the violets and merged into the sea of print frocks and floral scent.

The boy grinned at Dorothy. "5p," he said, "and pretty girls get an extra throw."

He held out a hand that was as large as her father's. A man's hand. She fumbled for a coin in her pocket and handed it to him. He piled six wooden balls into her arms. One tumbled out onto the floor. He picked it up and stretched out the front of his shirt towards her.

"Here," he said, "put them in here."

She dropped the balls into the scoop of his shirt and then threw each in turn at the china piled up on the shelves some twenty feet away. Each fell short, although the last dislodged a casserole dish that fell to the floor undamaged. The boy returned the dish to the shelf and, smiling, turned to the next girl in the queue.

* * * * *

Dorothy stretched out on her back on the slowly spinning roundabout in the community centre playground and shut her eyes. The rain had stopped and the weak sun was warm on her face. The only noise was the squeak of the swing chains and the clack-clack of the roundabout on the concrete.

The squeaking stopped. "You said the Girl Guides were a load of shit," Lilly said.

"Yeah, well, they still are. You're sure I won't have to wear a uniform?" She shuddered at the thought of the navy blue skirt and blouse and all those award badges.

"Not if you get a note from your mum saying you can't afford it."

"And you get to go Tree Sitting next month with the Venture Scouts, right?"

Lilly got off the swing and stepped onto the roundabout. "I think it's stupid. Sitting up a tree all night for charity. And in February. It'll be bloody freezing."

"Well, you don't have to go."

"I *can't* go. My mum won't let me." Lilly sat down. "Anyway, it's just boys being stupid. Some of them drink beer and pee off the platforms. Last year, they had a spitting contest. Sweet Jesus, they're like little kids."

Dorothy sat up and braked her foot against the concrete, slowing the roundabout. "Wasn't he the best-looking boy you've ever seen?" she asked.

"Who?"

She pulled the paper bag out of her pocket. "Do you want a bookmark?"

* * * * *

She sat on a pile of blue exercise mats in the Girl Guide Meeting Room at the back of the Scout hut in the village. She was working on her birding badge project, which involved making a kestrel from one of her Dad's old socks and a pile of chicken feathers.

"Dorothy Thompson, where is your uniform?" Mrs. Evans, troupe leader, sat on a stool underneath the medicine ball rack. Her blue guide cap was pinned into her thin grey hair, her huge breasts obscured by an array of badges.

"My mum said she can't afford a uniform," she lied. She didn't care what the other girls in the pokey room thought. She only had to last one more week as a guide, and then it was the Tree Sitting weekend.

"Then I need a note," Mrs. Evans said. "Or maybe one of you other guides can bring in an old uniform? Something you've grown out of?"

Dorothy turned back to her sock kestrel and daydreamed about the boy from the church fête. She'd found out his name was Chris Tendall, and that he went to Our Lady of the Holy Cross. She had looked up his address in the phone book and sure enough, it was a big swanky semi on Hangman's Lane. She'd then spent the following Saturday reading a magazine on a wall just down the street from his house.

When she first saw him, he was washing his father's bronze Mercedes. His little brother threw a bucket of water over him and his wet hair separated into fat curls, like puppy fur. He'd turned around quickly and smiled at her. She hadn't had time to look away, so she just tossed her head and hurried up the hill back towards the estate.

The next time she got off the school bus, he was waiting on the church wall for her.

* * * * *

She sat in the dining room practicing scales on the piano and listening to Mrs. O'Flannery talking to her mother at the kitchen door. Apparently, Lilly still hadn't been able to get permission to go Tree Sitting even though Mrs. Evans sent a note home saying it would be completely supervised. Mrs. O'Flannery said Lilly couldn't go, that there was no way she was going to trust a bunch of over-sexed adolescent boys with her fourteen-year-old daughter, and that she hoped Mrs. Thompson would follow suit. After all, it was just tempting fate putting teenage boys and girls together at night. Her mother said she'd consider it and shut the back door.

Dorothy closed her eyes and prayed that her mother wouldn't take Mrs. O'Flannery's advice. After all, she'd spent nearly a month making a kestrel out of a sock and was sick to death of feathers. She'd even had to sew the stupid Birding Badge to the sleeve of the blue cardigan she wore in lieu of a uniform.

Her mother came into the dining room and sat on the long bench beside her at the piano. Dorothy said nothing and started climbing slowly up through the scales again.

"I think the silly woman's got it the wrong way around." Her mother picked up the sock kestrel. "Given that girl's reputation, I'd say it was the boys who were in danger, not Lilly." She pressed her fingers to her forehead. "What with overbearing mothers, your father's trumpet playing and you murdering this piano, I think I'm coming down with a migraine."

Dorothy stopped playing. "Can I go then?" The permission slip and sponsorship form were propped up on top of the piano.

"Beats me why you want to sit in a tree house all night."

"It's not a tree house. It's a platform *in* a tree. And it's for charity."

Her mother put the kestrel on the top of the piano and lit a cigarette. "You say Brown Owl will be there?"

"That's for Brownies. We have a Troupe Leader."

"What about the boys? Will their Arkela be there?"

"Scout Master, Mum. It's a Scout Master."

"Oh, I don't know. It all sounds rather dull to me."

"I need it for my Camp Craft badge."

"I'll make a deal with you." Her mother picked up the permission form and took a pen from the pot next to the kestrel.

"What?"

"You promise not to make me any more chickens out of old socks, and I'll sign."

"Deal!"

Her mother signed the permission slip and jotted down an entry on the sponsorship form. "There you go," she said, blowing the ink dry. "There's fifty pence to start you off."

* * * * *

It was chilly, and Dorothy turned up the collar of Chris's jacket around her neck. She rubbed her hands together.

"You had to make it out of what?" Chris bounced a football from one knee to the other.

Dorothy snatched the ball and hid it behind her back. "One of my Dad's socks and some chicken feathers. I hate the Guides."

"You know," he said, "I never thought you looked like standard Girl Guide material." He lunged for the ball and pinned her against the boot of his father's Mercedes.

"Oh yeah?" she said. "And what do standard Girl Guides look like?"

"Not, little girl, like you." He bounced the ball sharply from between her hands and disappeared into the house.

* * * * *

Eight girls had managed to get permission to go on the Tree Sitting overnighter, and each slept bundled in her sleeping bag. Mrs Evans, after telling them about platform safety and how they'd have to wait until the morning if a "call of nature" came upon them, was snoring louder than anyone. Above Dorothy's head, through the tangle of bare branches, a slice of moon shone and a few dim stars pulsed, then faded away in the clouds. She could hear the boys sniggering from the platform in the next tree.

Mr. Avery, the Scout Master, barked at them to shut up. "You're not here to have fun!" he shouted. "You're here to be vigilant and learn from the experience."

They quieted down until one of them farted, and the whole tree erupted into hoots of laughter. She peered down into the darkness inside her sleeping bag and checked for what must have been the tenth time that her torch batteries were working.

Chris had told her that once everyone had gone to sleep they would both slip down out of the trees, and he'd show her the lake. He said there was a long-eared owl that flew low across the water at night, hunting for fish. She knew there wouldn't be, that long-eared owls lived near the coast and didn't eat fish. After all, she had the badge to prove it. He said he would shine his torch up into the canopy of branches three times to tell her when to climb down and meet him.

She was almost asleep when she saw the beam light the underside of the boughs. She quietly climbed down the ladder into the dark woods below.

* * * * *

His arm around her shoulder was heavy, and his hand felt warm through her jumper.

"Are you cold?" he asked.

She nodded. He shrugged off his leather bomber jacket and draped it carefully around her shoulders. As she pulled up the zipper, he lifted her chin with his finger. His eyes were as soft as they had been at the fête, and she felt the heat of his wide mouth upon her lips. The leaf litter was damp beneath her, and a tree root dug into her shoulder. He ran his fingers across her collarbone underneath her jumper, pushing the bra strap off her shoulder. She concentrated on his lips, on his tongue, insistent in her mouth and on the cold cry of an owl above them in the willows that grew by the river's edge. She listened again. A tawny owl. She could see the sliver of moon reflected in the dark span of water, a sudden absence of stars. She closed her eyes and heard the unmistakable drizzle of a Boy Scout urinating off the edge of the tree platform high in the trees behind them.

God's got big hands. When we die, we get to sit on them. Girls on his left hand, and boys on his right. Like in school assembly. God's hands have to be as big as arm-chairs. Or even bigger, just in case really fat people with big bums die.

Or maybe he's got normal grown-up hands, and we shrink down into little tiny angels. Like Tinkerbell. Or my Barbie.

When you sit in his hands, you tell him all the bad things you've done, and he writes them down in his diary. It's got a lock on it like Dorothy's. If you've done too many bad things, he turns his hand over and drops you into hell.

Satan's a falling angel and that's why God never stands up. He just sits in his big throne made out of telegraph poles and cassocks. He can't risk falling over, because he might slip off the cloud and fall into Hell like Satan did.

He should get a stick like the one we got our gran. Or a walking frame.

Sticklebacks

✳

Gerald Damson sat at the dining room table and studied the upright piano in the corner of the room. He'd never learnt to play the thing, but since it didn't make the reserve price at the creditors' auction, he'd brought it with them to Stanley Close. The dark rosewood piano, with its turned legs and front panel inlaid with bright foliage and flowers, seemed out of place in the shabby little room. It was missing its upholstered bench. A woman at the auction had confided in him that it would make a nice window seat for her conservatory and had stolen it for the sum of forty pounds. The piano had been benchless now for five months.

He picked up his chair and set it in front of the piano. He sat down, shut his eyes, and placed his hands palm-down on the smooth key cover. Outside, he could hear the blue tits bickering over the pork rind Pamela had hung from a nail on the shed door. "Tsee-tsee-tsu-tsuhuhu! Tsee-tsee-tsu-tsuhuhu!" All that racket for rancid pork rind! Through the thin wall, he could hear his wife talking to the rent man in the kitchen. Her voice was low, like the hum of distant traffic.

He always stayed in the dining room while she paid the weekly rent. It wasn't that he disliked talking to the rent man.

It was the fact that seeing her hand over the money made their situation real. He was no longer Mr. Damson of The Grange, West Barrington. He was just another tenant on the sprawling Bishop's Croft council housing estate.

He opened his eyes and eased up the rosewood cover. A blue metal cash box sat on the top of the keys. Seven slots. Six marked neatly with sticky labels: *Gas. Electric. Food. Clothes. Rent. Catalogue.* He snapped open the lid, ran his finger over the coins and notes in each compartment, and considered how times had changed. Gone were the afternoons in his panelled office above the factory floor, watching his workforce pack surgical equipment into shiny red *Damson Instrument* boxes. Gone were the executive lunches with customers. The creditors had taken everything. The Jaguar, Pamela's jewellery, even his golf clubs. Everything. And now he worked forty hours a week at Rokers, balancing columns of figures as relevant to him as telephone numbers in a phone directory.

He counted the money in the unmarked compartment. Two pounds, fifty-five pence in small coins: pennies, ten pence pieces, a couple of shiny fifties. Each coin was gleaned through sacrifice. Last week, the weather had been unusually clement for March, so he had walked to work, saving pennies on the bus fare. Rather than joining the other office workers in the canteen for lunch and tea breaks, he took sandwiches to work. He opted out of the tea club and used his own teabags, making endless pots of tea in the pokey kitchenette behind the storeroom. The coins added up.

And there were sacrifices outside work too. He no longer subscribed to *The Times*. Instead, he called at the library on the way home from work and read the communal copy. The young librarian always smiled at him and now, when he sat down at the desk beneath the signed photograph of the Witford Football team, the paper would be there waiting for him. Sometimes he wished he could just stay there and hide among all the books and magazines. He fantasized about the librarian with her short brown hair and Indian-print skirts.

He swapped the coins for two pound notes from *Food* and slipped the cash in his trouser pocket. Pamela's brittle laughter sifted through from the kitchen. Strange how she often laughed with the rent man, even though she told Gerald she didn't like him. She said when he looked at her, she felt naked. It was something, she said, about the way he smiled. Gerald told her she was imagining things. She probably wasn't, but what could he do about it?

There had been a time when she loved him with a hunger. He ran his finger silently across the creamy piano keys and remembered her lying naked on the sofa, the fondue set sitting on the hearth, its shining bowl full of melted chocolate. He smiled at the memory, but the smile didn't linger. Since the creditors, there had been no more chocolate.

He shut the cash box and slid it back beneath the rosewood lid for safekeeping. Its corner hit one of the ebony keys and a fractured note hovered like a question in the air. The voices continued from the kitchen, oblivious to the interruption.

What were they talking about that was so funny? He stood up slowly, and hugging close to the wall, crept silently towards the kitchen. He stopped at the door and listened, the paintwork cold against his ear. She laughed again, a spread-legged kind of laugh. For a moment, it made him feel desperately sad. It made him think of the fondue set on the hearth, full of warm, thick chocolate. Then he tipped over into feeling very frightened. He thumped down on the door handle and burst into the kitchen, his rubber-soled slippers screeching across the linoleum.

Pamela stared at him from the small kitchen table in the centre of the room. She held a sugar cube in the jaws of the silver tongs over the rent man's cup of tea.

"I've got to go out," Gerald said.

Neither of them spoke. They just sat there—the rent man looking at Pamela and Pamela holding the tongs.

"I've got to go into town," he said, more to the rent man than to his wife. "I have a luncheon appointment . . . in Soho."

"That's nice, dear," his wife said, dropping the cube into the rent man's tea.

He gripped the back of her chair. "Aren't you in a hurry?" he said to the man with the clipboard.

The rent man picked up the spoon from his saucer and pointed it at Gerald. "Never too much in a hurry for a lady as lovely as your wife, Mr. Damson. I was just telling her what a lucky man you are." He stirred his tea. The spoon clattered against his cup, and splashed tea on a small pile of pound notes on the table.

Gerald glared at the man, taking in the suit with its wide lapels, the polished brown laceups with stacked Cuban heels. He kissed his wife noisily on the cheek. "I'll be back later," he said. She didn't reply, merely dabbed her face with the hem of her apron and smiled back at the rent man. Gerald walked through to the hall, grabbed his jacket from the rack and opened the front door.

"Slippers, Gerald," his wife called. He looked down at the tartan slip-ons. He kicked them off and slid his feet into a pair of leather brogues on the mat. He pulled the door shut behind him with a click and heard the rent man's laugh, a low rumble.

On the circular Green in the centre of Stanley Close, a knot of girls played. They were gathering up piles of clippings left by the council mowers' first cut of the year and forming them into grass walls. Each child was engrossed with the construction of her own home: a palace, a flat in Hampstead, a detached house in Ruislip. He skirted around the children, mown grass clinging to his shoes and lining his trouser turn-ups. When he reached the rose bushes at the edge of the Green, he was seized with a desire to turn back and join them, to gather up armfuls of his own clippings and build a little square house out there on the grass. One room, just big enough for him and Pamela. No rent man, no creditors, no tin cashbox. The idea made him smile and stayed with him all the way into London on the twelve-o-seven to Euston.

* * * * *

At Euston Central, he pushed through the double glass station doors and joined the lunchtime throng on the Concourse. He crossed the busy road at the traffic lights and stood outside the small Italian restaurant whose iron vine-encircled sign read "La Bellagio." The air was thick with the smell of exhaust from the buses, cars, and black cabs. He opened Bellagio's door and slipped thankfully into the dark interior, taking a seat towards the back of the restaurant.

A man wearing a cream and blue striped duck apron emerged from the kitchen and seeing Gerald, picked up a menu from the stand, licked his pencil and hurried to the table.

"Ah, *buon giorno*, Signor Damsons. You are, as they say, regular as clockwork, no?"

Gerald smiled and waved away the menu. "Hello, Vincenzo. How could I ever be late for a Bellagio feast!"

"Ah, for feasts you should come to Sicily! Where the grapes and the women are ripe and warm, yes!"

He smiled again. "I wish I had the time, Vincenzo."

"Time! When is there ever enough? But, since we are stuck here in London, what can I bring you?"

"I'll have my usual. You have the veal?"

"Ah, we have veal to cry over! Tears of pure joy!" He tucked the menu under his arm. "I have veal grilled over rosemary which has sat for a day in the finest cold-press olive oil and lemon marinade."

"Then the veal," replied Gerald.

Vincenzo nodded and bustled back to the kitchen, his tie hooked over his shoulder. He turned. "Signor Damsons, you would like a glass of our own Frascatti?"

"Of course, Vincenzo. Of course."

* * * * *

The veal was delicious. Tender and cooked to perfection as it was every Saturday. He had been lunching at Vincenzo's for over ten years, enjoying the tender veal and entertaining his clients. He pushed his plate away and savoured the final drops of the cold Frascatti, its dry notes cutting through the richness that lingered in his mouth.

"The veal was good, yes?" Vincenzo picked up the plate.

"The veal was very good. Tell your chef he surpassed himself. Join me for a liqueur?"

Vincenzo shook his head as he did every Saturday. "You don't need to do that, Signor Damsons. I know you are a busy man, and I am just a humble waiter who knows nothing."

Gerald smiled. "No, I insist. You keep me in touch with the world, my friend. Please."

Vincenzo bowed and returned minutes later with a tray holding two glasses of Sambuca and the bill in a saucer. He sat down, took a glossy brown coffee bean from the saucer and dropped it into Gerald's shot glass. The rich anise aroma hung between the two men.

"For luck," he said. "Not that a man like you needs to rely on luck. *Alla salute!*" They chinked glasses across the table and drained them in one swallow.

Vincenzo handed Gerald a cigar, then lit it for him. "So, how is business?" he asked. "How are your scalpels selling today?"

"I must say, I am cutting quite a swathe through the competition." Both men laughed.

Vincenzo took a cigarette from his packet. "Ah, your workers are lucky to have such a gentleman in charge. My father, he used to say it takes a real gentleman to be a great boss. From the old families down to the shoe-shiners—manners—they make the man."

"I agree. I think it matters. It gives the men something to . . . respect." Gerald drew deep on his cigar. "But you are a man of business, Vincenzo." He gestured to the restaurant around him. "You know how lonely it gets at the top."

The Italian nodded gravely. "I cannot get the staff. The people they send me are pigs! Long-haired poofs! All of them. I have to send home, bring my nephews here. You have good men at the factory, no?"

"Oh yes. I am blessed with my workforce. They love me, you see. They look up to me."

Both men sat in companionable silence, their empty glasses touching on the table and Gerald's cigar smoke mingling with the haze from Vincenzo's cigarette. He glanced at the bill and placed two pounds, fifty-five pence on the saucer. The Italian smiled.

* * * * *

Gerald stepped out onto the platform at Bishop's Croft railway station. Behind him, the anonymous train pulled out and, gathering speed, disappeared with a rising scream behind the bare, brown bones of Tenner's Wood.

He decided to walk back along the canal to Stanley Close. It would save him the bus fare, and the longer he went without human contact, the longer his contentment lasted. He handed the ticket collector his stub and crossed the quiet lane to the footpath that led to the Grand Union.

He walked slowly along the gravel towpath, skirting the anglers hunched over their rods and thermos flasks of coffee, their breath blooming over the dark, oiled water. He remembered his collection of antique fishing reels. All of them gone to the bank. Except the Nottingham Mahogany. That had been an anniversary present for Pamela and consequently was outside the creditors' grasp.

At the bridge that marked the beginning of the long hill away from the canal and back up to the estate, a young girl sat at the edge of the towpath. She dangled her foot in the murky water and trailed a bamboo-handled fishing net across the surface. A jam jar sat next to her. Inside, brown spotted stickle-backs mouthed the glass. As he passed her, she looked up from the water and smiled.

"Hello, Mr. Angelfish," she said.

He stopped. "I'm sorry. Are you talking to me?"

"Yep," she said and lifted her foot from the water, pulled off her plimsoll and emptied it into the jam jar. The fish disappeared in a swirl of mud and pondweed. She dipped her bare foot back into the water.

He looked closer and recognised her as the Thompson girl. Tot Thompson from next door.

"Why do you call me Mr. Angelfish?" he said, leaning against the curved brickwork of the bridge.

She put the shoe upside down on the gravel and turned back to her net and the canal full of minnows and sticklebacks. "My dad had a fish who looked like you. A bit, anyway." Her bare foot shone almost luminous through the brown water. "Want some Hubba Bubba?" she said and thrust a packet of bubble gum towards him.

He shook his head.

She shrugged and placed a pink round of gum in her mouth. "My dad said you had a big factory, but you lost all your money to the Inland Revenue, and that's why you live next door. Do you play that piano?"

He wondered how she knew about the piano.

"I saw the men bring it in." She shook the net, and skeins of weed flew across the surface of the water, then disappeared on the opposite bank.

"Look how far that weed went!" she said. "Bloody far!" She lifted her foot from the water, wiped it on her discarded jacket, and then crammed it back into the canvas shoe beside her. She picked up the jam jar and peered through the glass. "Seven," she counted and tied a length of string around the neck of the jar. "Do you come here every Saturday?" She checked the fish again, her mouth moving as she silently recounted.

"No," he said. "Er, yes. Not here, exactly. But somewhere else."

"I used to go horse riding on Saturdays, but I've given it up. Just for a while." She stood up and knocked the gravel from her knees. "Can you keep a secret?" she asked, shrugging on the pink anorak.

He picked up her net and inspected the nylon for holes. "Oh yes, I'm really rather good at keeping secrets." He handed it to her. "That's a fine fishing net."

"I know," she said, resting it over her shoulder. "You can get cheap ones, but Dorothy says that if a thing's worth doing, it's worth doing well. And I can't do it well with a crappy net."

"Dorothy?"

"My sister. She's in the Guides, and they know all about that kind of thing . . . birds and sewing and that." She pulled up her socks and straightened her skirt. "Do you want to hear my secret?" she said.

"Go on then."

"My Dad's going to leave us and go to America. He said he'd send me a snow globe and not to tell mum, but I made a deal with God so he wouldn't go."

He felt the damp from the brickwork seeping through his thin jacket. He coughed. "Er, if this is a really complicated secret, would you mind if we sat down on that bench over there?"

She nodded and the pair of them moved out from under the shadow of the bridge and sat down on the wooden bench. She continued. "I said that since he loves little children and wants them all for sunbeams, I'd be a sunbeam if he stops my dad from going to America to play the trumpet." She picked at a scab on her knee. "And then Lilly O'Flannery said you can't just ask God for things. You have to promise something in return. She told me all about the lady saints and how they made sacrifices for their faith and stuff. Like having nails stuck in their ears or doing something they're really good at, like singing or playing the harp, but forever." She flicked the picked scab onto the gravel. "All I can do really well is catch fish, and God likes fish, right?"

He shook his head. "You're losing me."

"You know! All that stuff with the fishes and the bread rolls. Anyway, I did a deal and said that I'd catch seven stickle-backs for seven Saturdays and sacrifice them to God if he'd stop my dad going to America."

"Sacrifice them?"

She wrinkled her nose. "Yeah, it's a bit icky. I'm going to squish them with a house brick." He winced. "Do you think it'll work?" she asked.

"I don't know."

"You won't tell anyone, will you? It won't work if it's not a secret."

He nodded.

She stood and picked up the jar of sticklebacks and walked off down the towpath. Suddenly, she stopped and turned back. "Do you play that piano?" she asked.

"No," he said. "I never learnt."

"Well, excuse my French," she said. "But that's bloody stupid. Like . . . having it and not playing it." She slung the net over the other shoulder. "I could teach you, if you want. I know "Chopsticks" all the way through."

He looked at the girl on the towpath. Water and pondweed dripped from the net across her shoulder, and she and the seven sticklebacks seemed to be waiting for an answer. "That would be lovely," he said. "Thank you."

She shrugged her shoulders and blew a huge pink bubble.

"S'all right, Mr. Angelfish," she said, turning once again and heading off down the towpath with her fish. "Any time."

SPRING 1972

The man who owns this campsite calls me "Treasure" and gives me a box of chocolate Poppets every morning when we leave for the beach. I make myself wait until I can see the sand dunes before I stick my thumb through the opening in the side of the box and roll one out onto my tongue. You can't bite them. You have to suck.

Some have got orange cream in the middle or honeycomb. But some, and there's not many, have got green mint. If I get a minty, I spit it back in the box.

When mum and dad are asleep, and Dorothy's reading her magazines, I dig a BIG hole. Then I get in and pull all the sand back over me. Not right over because that's how people suffocate; I leave my head and one arm sticking out.

When it's just waves and seagulls and my dad snoring, I shut my eyes and wait. I wait until the sun makes my hair boil and my eyelids shine. Then I pour the minties into my mouth. All at once.

There's something about listening to the waves and sucking a mouthful of minties. I don't know what it is. It's just something . . . bigger.

The Match

❊

Tot Thompson suffered from fits. Not great roll-around fits, but quiet ones. Sometimes, friends thought she was only daydreaming. Before they found out about the fits, they'd shake her and shout in her ears. They thought she was being weird. Until her mother put them right.

"Tot has fits," she told them. "They're nothing to be scared of, but you must run and fetch me or her father if you think she's having one." The other kids looked at Tot as if she were a liability. A glass child.

At first, life had been a nightmare. She'd be watching ants under a hedge or lying in the grass listening for worms and someone would go running to her parents, and she'd be whisked up and inspected for signs of seizure. So, she took to humming loudly. And smiling on the basis that people having fits weren't happy. It seemed to work.

Today, she was poking at a cigarette end in the gutter with a twig and humming the theme tune to *Match of the Day*, just so that anybody watching would know she was only being quiet and wasn't having a fit. Seamus O'Flannery, Stanley Close's very own retard, sat on the pavement next to her. He was twelve and too old for her to play with, but she didn't mind him sitting there. She liked to listen to him breathe. It sounded like he had soup up his nose. When he got excited or angry, he'd yap like the Deepens's greyhound.

She was cold and wished the two boys on the Green would hurry up and choose their teams. She zipped up her pink anorak, her new one with embroidered birds, and pulled up the hood. Seamus's brother, Michael, stood in conference with Nigel Deepens, no doubt discussing which team would play in which direction. A cluster of boys stood around the telegraph pole on the edge of the Green trying not to look concerned about who got picked first . . . or last. Michael held the football, an Adidas Telstar, securely under his arm. It was his ball, and that meant to anyone who knew the rules that he would pick first.

Tot was good at football. She didn't toe punt the ball like most girls. She could kick it with the side of her foot and her father said she had a good eye. She hoped she wouldn't get picked last. She really hoped she wouldn't get picked after Seamus.

* * * * *

```
    My brother, Michael, is a Superstar
and has the best football in the world.
The girl has pretty birds on her sleeves.
They are flying on pink, but there are no
sounds. Just green birds with yellow beaks
floating on her arms. I'm hungry. I fed
my breakfast to the painted bird on the
tablemat. I always feed the bird because
he has no legs. Birds with no legs cannot
catch their own worms. They are not quick
enough. She has birds on her sleeves, and
on the back there is a big bird. It is the
bird in my book. It has flown from my book
and landed on her jacket. I hope he comes
```

```
back. He must or else the words will be
lonely and they will have to talk about
something else, about another animal. A
dog. A dog with teeth. I can't have a dog.
Mummy says they have to have a licence
and it's enough to look after a Retard
without having hair on the carpet. My hair
is white, like Jesus's hair on the cross
in the church near our school. The man in
mauve says Jesus loves me and knows about
every sparrow. She doesn't have sparrows
on her arms. Hers are green and sparrows
are dirty. Michael has the best football
in the world.
```

* * * * *

She stood up, brushed the cold of the kerb off her backside, and picked a long spray of privet from the hedge. She pulled off all the leaves and wound it into a loop. She watched the boys on the Green.

"I'll have Craig," Michael said and Craig walked out from the knot of boys, his bony shoulders held back and a smile as wide as a church door. Nigel kicked at the grass and looked the other kids over.

"Kenny then." Kenny followed suit and stood next to Nigel.

She watched the routine. Always the same. Craig and Kenny were picked first. They were the biggest and Craig had access to his father's dirty magazines. She wanted Nigel to pick her. She'd practiced kissing her arm in her bedroom and dribbling the ball in the back garden. She was good at both, although her ball control needed a little more work. But her kissing was the business. Not too wet, and she'd learnt not to suck. No tongues, though. No way. She'd heard Lilly telling Dorothy that you had to save something for afters. She wasn't

too sure what afters were, or how she would manage to com-
bine football and kissing, but she felt sure that something
would come to her if he'd only pick her for his team. He'd be
gob smacked. A good dribbler and a brilliant kisser. He only
had to pick her to find out.

She ran her tongue over her teeth to make sure that Kit-
the-Shit wasn't about to turn up. Kit wasn't a boy. It was her
name for the fits. Her mum had told her all about the bad
epileptic brain things on bicycles and the goodies on chemical
horses, but she didn't buy all that. Kit-the-Shit, or Kit-the-
Fit as she referred to him at home, was just a bully who came
round now and then and butted in. She imagined him as being
Swedish or Norwegian. Not dishy like Bjorn Borg, but ugly—a
skinny boy with a pointed head and big bulging blue eyes. Kit
always threw pennies in her mouth before he started shaking
her. Their metal taste would stick to her teeth, and she'd know
he was hanging around somewhere. But she was all right for
now. Her mouth tasted minty.

She walked along the hedges that edged each square front
garden and swiped the privet loop through the spiders' webs
hanging across the tightly packed leaves. She held the web loop
up to the sky. It sparkled.

* * * * *

My brother Michael is King. Mummy
loves him and makes sure he has chocolate
'Breakaways' in his lunch box. I've seen
her put them in. I get chocolate-spread
sandwiches and long slices of carrot to
keep my teeth white. She says they make me
see in the dark, but it doesn't work. I
still can't see the insects that crawl in
under our bedroom door. I can hear them.
They rub their ears together, and their
sharp mouths tell me my brother loves me

and that one day we will all live together
in a big house in the city. I have seen
the city on the television. There are
bright lights on chains that hang around
the tops of houses. Big houses whose roofs
are up in the sky, in the stars. There are
hundreds of bedrooms in these houses. The
man in mauve says there are many rooms in
Jesus's house. Jesus lives in the city.
He lives in Manchester. Michael and I
will live in one of those rooms and we
will have lambs for pets and pockets full
of little birds. They will perch on wire
clothes hangers and lay their eggs in
my sock drawer. Baby birds—canaries and
budgerigars—will sing each morning as I
open the door and take out my school uniform. I will go to the school in the city
with Michael and we will do woodwork.
Mummy won't let me do woodwork. Brother
Jenkins says I will cut my bloody arm off.
But Michael will save me. Michael will
make sure I don't cut my bloody arm off.

* * * * *

She watched the group of boys on the grass. There were
only three who hadn't been picked: Allan, Melvyn, and Keesal.
Allan and Melvyn were digging holes in the dirt with a penknife, and Keesal, a dark-skinned boy with short trousers, stood
apart from the group, his school tie hanging out of his pocket.
    Keesal hadn't lived in Stanley Close very long. Her dad told
her Keesal was Indian and that was why he had a brown face
like the coalman. The other boys didn't like him. She thought
they were complete spanners for picking on him and calling him
names like Paki Wacky and Punka Wallah. After all, Stanley

Close now had its very own Indian. He didn't have a piebald pony like Geronimo, or a headdress made from deerskin and eagle feathers, but he was still an Indian.

She wondered why he came out to play in the holidays with his school tie in his pocket. She wondered a lot about Keesal and Keesal's house. His mother never came outside, and in the evening, strange smells fell from their kitchen window and wafted down the alley. It smelt like the Tiger of Bengal take-away in the village. She imagined the Patel dining room. It would have red and gold furry wallpaper and little china elephant salt and pepper shakers. In the corner, Keesal's dad would play a sitar like Labi Sifri, and his music would seep down the alley alongside the smell of their dinner.

Michael had picked Allan, and now his team was limbering up, the boys stretching their skinny, white legs and bouncing the ball to each other with their knees. Nigel took Keesal and got Melvyn thrown in for free. Melvyn wasn't crippled. He just woke up one morning and his legs didn't work properly. Tot thought they'd probably start working again later in the summer. She had lost her voice for a week once, and then it came back. Her father said it was a godsend it had stayed away as long as it had.

"Tot," Michael said. "I'll have Tot." Bugger. She didn't want to play on his team. She wanted to play on Nigel's. She stood up and rubbed her hands warm on the front of her trousers. At least she got picked before Seamus.

* * * * *

He picked her. My brother picked the
girl with the birds on her arms. It must
be the birds. How could you not want a
girl with birds on her arms? I am growing
feathers. I have quills under my arms and
between my legs. It feels like Easter when
I scratch them. Soon they will become

```
feathers, and I will be able to fly away
to the city. Michael has feathers. I have
seen them. Black curly feathers like Gran-
dad's bantams.
```
"Oi, Retard! Over here. You can be a goalpost."
```
       I don't want to be a goalpost. I want
to be with my brother, the two of us flying
through the air to the city.
```

* * * * *

What the hell is that loony doing, Tot wondered. She watched Seamus jumping up and down on the pavement, a look of intense concentration on his face. Nigel marched across to the two heaps of jackets that made up his team's goal. He looked fed up at the prospect of Seamus in the game, even as a goalpost. He pulled off his jumper and threw it on the pile. Underneath, he wore a dark blue Fred Perry. She loved his clothes. He was a real skinhead, and she was angry that her mum had given Dorothy's too-small tonic-silk skirt to Lilly O'Flannery. If Tot had worn that skirt today, Nigel would have picked her. She could have stood on the pavement, turning this way and that, and he would have been stunned by the way her skinhead skirt flashed blue then green. Now she was in Michael's team and Lilly had the skirt and Nigel would never know.

"Come on then, if you're playing!" Michael stood at the opposite side of the green with his hands on his hips. "Are you playing or what?" She stood up and handed the privet spider web loop to Seamus, who had stopped jumping. He took it and his hands felt warm and damp on her fingers. She flinched and rubbed them up and down on her jacket. She watched him put the loop up to his face and press his nose through the webs. Loonie, she thought and walked across the road to join the rest of her team.

* * * * *

I am a Retard. I like the sound but I
know it means a bad thing. But Michael
doesn't stop them saying it, so he must
know a good way of being a Retard. She's
given me soft. The girl with the birds has
given me softness and now I'm breathing
it. On the loop, it is white with spiders,
but in my head, in my breath, it is green
like flame from bottles on a bonfire. I have
green in my head, and when she rubbed the
birds on her coat, they sang. They called
to the arm birds and they all began to
sing. Father George showed me a picture of
Saint Assisi in the big book. The birds
love him and they all live in the folds
of his sleeves. Birds sleeping in the
fall of his brown sleeves. They sing to
me when the sun goes to sleep. I can hear
them from the back lawn. Saint Assisi is
standing by the bird table, and they are
all singing. In the city, I am going to
buy a Ben Sherman like Michael's and leave
the cuffs unbuttoned. I will take roosting
birds from the eaves and stand in other
Retards' gardens. I will send music to
them. Music will sift through the cracks
in their window frames, just like it does
through mine.

* * * * *

Keesal headed the ball to Tot, and she stopped it on her
knee, bouncing it up into the air, keeping one eye on the ball
and one on Nigel. He wasn't looking, but there was time. Fifteen minutes each way. She pondered the strategy of a tackle.
If she were to throw herself at him when he had the ball, they

might land in a tangle in the grass and accidentally she could press her lips to his and they would kiss. He would know that underneath her pink anorak with the stupid embroidered birds, she was a real skinhead girl, and he might fall in love with her there and then. Or maybe she could get a concussion, and since he was the oldest boy on the Green, he would have to go in the ambulance with her and he would hold her hand. She kicked the ball to Melvyn, who stopped it dead with the rubber bung on the end of his wooden crutch.

Neat move, she thought, just as Kit-the-Shit arrived. He appeared in front of her, smiling, and tossed a handful of coins in her mouth. There was nothing she could do apart from move them around with her tongue, each penny coating her teeth with metal. She couldn't see Kit any more, but he was there. He was turning the volume up and down on the afternoon. Nigel was shouting and then whispering. Up on the telegraph pole, a string of swallows screamed at her and then mouthed their songs so quietly, she couldn't make out what they were saying. She caught snatches of Michael shouting at Seamus and could see the loony jumping up and down on the pavement again. But he was staying in the air for too long. He looked like he was ascending, like Jesus, and then the grass stopped being grass. The boys lifted their legs in a sea of green soap, and the sky began to shut down. Her mouth was full of pennies and she floated in the green light of the grass. Warmth flooded her thighs, and the sounds of Stanley Close were like the sounds of a party downstairs when it's late and you're too tired to concentrate and someone has shut the bedroom door. Just some words come through, stumbling up the stairs. She could hear her father playing trumpet in the spare room. She could see Seamus flying across the grass. Seamus swooping with the swallows.

* * * * *

The birds are dying! She's crushing
them, mangling their feathers in the

ground. They're not her birds to crush.
I can't undo her zipper. Mummy has sewed
Velcro into my jacket because she knows
I can't do zips, and now the birds have
stopped singing. There is just the yellow
noise from the window at number seventeen.
The man with the golden metal singing
through that window. The words say that
he can save the birds. He is not a Saint,
but he is the girl's Daddy, like mine,
but hers is here and mine is living in
the city. Not in a house of many rooms,
like the one Michael and I are going to
live in, but in the Big House. There are
no lights on chains in the Big House, but
Michael says there are chains and Mummy
says she is chained to the man in the Big
House. MAN! THE LITTLE BIRD IS DYING! I
have these words and throw them at the
window with the yellow song. MAN, THE GIRL
IS CRUSHING ALL THE BIRDS! COME QUICK!
COME SAVE THE BIRDS! Nigel is screaming at
me. He doesn't know about the man with the
yellow noise and the birds drowning in the
sea of green. This door is blue and I have
lost my loop of soft. Come down, Man, and
open your door. Unzip her jacket and let
the birds go. Let them go.

* * * * *

Tot could feel the urine soaking through her trousers and
seeping up the back of her anorak. Her father unzipped her
jacket, took it off, and threw it on the grass. He shook out a
tartan blanket, and as he picked her up in his arms, he wrapped
it around her. She couldn't open her eyes or stop her one free

arm waving like a flag around her head. He held her close to his chest. Her mouth opened and shut, and then a stream of noise hit the air. "NOT PLAYING . . . NOT PLAYING . . . NOT PLAYING" she said, over and over again. He stroked her hair and carried her back across the grass to seventeen Stanley Close.

Seamus followed them, holding her pink jacket by the cuffs in front of him, as if it were a banner or a dance partner. Tot's father stood in the entranceway to their front garden, leaning against the replica Victorian gaslight and gently rocking her against his chest. He turned around and looked at the boy holding her jacket in his hands. He smiled and pulled a fifty pence piece from his trouser pocket.

"For calling me, son," he said. "For coming to get me."

Seamus draped the jacket gently over the privet hedge, took the coin, and dropped it in his pocket.

Nigel stood behind him and slapped him affectionately on the back. "Nice one, Loon!" he said. "Nice one!" He turned to Tot's father. "Will she be alright, Mr. Thompson?"

Tot smiled into her father's shoulder as Mr. Thompson nodded. Seamus skipped back across the grass to hand his brother the coin, his head full of birds singing "Seamus! Seamus!" from the privet hedge.

When "The Blue Notes" are playing up The Eagle on a Friday night, Uncle Ernie baby-sits. Mum says we're to do Fuzzy Felts or Spirograph until bedtime. But we don't.

Uncle Ernie's like Trampus off The Virginian. He doesn't ride a horse or wear a hat or anything, but he walks like a cowboy, and he's braver than anyone I know. Even my Dad.

Ernie says John Wayne never did Fuzzy Felts. So he takes us up to the big hill behind the woods where all the Dads put their clippings. Up there, it's like being on our shed roof, but higher. The grass is as sharp as wire. Sometimes, when it's windy, I can't hear anything. If I open my mouth, the wind gets in, and I feel like there's a train in my chest. I can't speak. It's like I swallowed God.

Uncle Ernie plays Pooh Darts, but only if we promise not to tell. Me and Dorothy sit with our mouths open, and he throws rabbit pooh at us. The one who catches the most in her mouth wins. Dorothy spits hers out, but I pack mine in my cheeks with my tongue. When I win, it makes Uncle Ernie laugh.

I like it when he laughs. It's how people laugh on the telly, but he's sitting right next to me.

Crystal Palace

❊

All of the world hummed and throbbed around the two girls as they made dinner invitations at the Wrights' formica-topped kitchen table. The washing machine rumbled its way through a load of bed sheets and crept an inch or two across the linoleum floor with each spin. Roger, the family dog, growled and groaned a dog dream from his basket below the table, and Stacey's father's work overalls hung dripping from a wire hanger above the boiler. Drops of water bubbled and hissed on the cast-iron boiler lid and the gently rising steam gathering above the back door. From the oven, a dim light shone illuminating a chocolate sponge cake, which Stacey's mother hoped would be ready in plenty of time before the scheduled power cut at seven o'clock that night. The steady sounds of the washing machine rumbling and squeaking its way across the kitchen floor and the ticking oven timer were accompanied by a tattoo of rain on the kitchen window and the squeak-squeak of pencils on paper.

At the foot of the boiler were Stacey's father's best shoes, each stuffed with newspaper. He'd walked to a union meeting in the rain that morning and had left them there to dry. Next to the shoes was a box of yellow handbills, each sheet calling for solidarity in support of the miners' strike.

Stacey's best friend, Tot, sat closest to the washing machine. Every few minutes, she pushed the creeping top loader back towards the sink, then returned to her colouring. The tip of her tongue stuck out from between her lips as she concentrated all her effort on keeping the brown crayon shading inside the pit pony outline that Stacey had drawn in black felt-tip. She tapped her foot on the floor in time with the ticking timer. She was wearing her older sister's lime green platform shoes.

Stacey looked at the shoes. Janine never let her borrow anything. "Does Dorothy let you wear her stuff?" she asked. Tot shook her head. "She'll kill you when she finds out."

"She won't find out," Tot replied. "I'm extra careful."

"How do you mean?"

Without looking up from her drawing, Tot pulled two plastic carrier bags from her pockets. "I stick 'em over the shoes so I don't get any dirt or grass on them." Tot sat back in her chair and smoothed out the piece of paper on the kitchen table. "So what do I write? Support the miners?"

"No. Nothing," Stacey said. "I'm the oldest, so I'm doing the middle bit." She picked up an uppercase rubber "P" from the tin in front of her and squeezed it into the plastic printer's stick. She inked the stick, then pressed it against a sheet of paper.

Tot slid off the chair and disappeared under the table. "My sister doesn't notice anything anymore. She's got a boyfriend. He's a Venture Scout," she said, her voice distant and muffled. "Have you got a boyfriend, Stacey?"

"I'm not allowed yet. I'm only ten. Anyway, I wouldn't tell you if I did have one." She wiped the printer's stick on a sheet of kitchen roll.

Tot reappeared in her chair. "Dorothy won't play with me no more," she said, prising up a corner of the sticky-back plastic table cover. "She says I'm too . . . immature."

Stacey blew on the sheet of paper.

"What's immature mean?" Tot asked.

"I think it's when you're too little to understand stuff."

"I like playing with you. You tell me things."

"We're not playing," Stacey said. "I'm too old to play with eight-year-olds like you."

"You're only like two Christmases and two birthdays and holidays older than me. Anyway," Tot grasped the corner of the table firmly between her teeth, "hnnnt arrrrr 'eee ' 'oing 'ow 'en?"

"What?"

Tot stopped chewing on the corner of the table. "What are we now doing then?"

"This isn't playing. We're supporting the miners." Stacey held her half of the invitation up to the light from the kitchen window.

"What does it say? Read it to me."

"It says, 'Stacey Wright and Tot Thompson invite their mums and dads to tea at Stacey's house tonite. There will be emergency lights and gin rummy. RSVP.'"

"Can I see it?" Tot said.

She handed over the sheet of paper. Tot read it, her lips moving over every word. "You haven't said anything about the miners."

"We don't have to. There's a pit pony on the front and my dad says, 'Softly Softly Catch The Monkey.'"

"What the bugger does that mean?"

"I don't know, but he always says it and then he taps his nose. I think it means that you have to be crafty. Anyway, he knows everything there is to know about the strike. If we can get your mum and dad here, my dad'll say all the stuff about the miners."

"My mum says it's a bloody disgrace," said Tot, handing the sheet back to Stacey.

"That's because she doesn't know about it. My dad'll tell her, and then she'll let you put posters up in your windows." Stacey put both sheets together. "We just need to staple this in the middle, and then you can give it to your mum."

"You don't spell tonight like that."

"I know. But I haven't got any g's and anyway, they spell it like that in America." Stacey tapped the edges of the paper sheets on the table.

"My dad's going . . ."

"Going where?" Stacey asked.

"Doesn't matter. What does RSVP mean?"

"It means say if you can come or not." Stacey stapled both sheets together, then folded them in half.

"Why don't you just put that, then?"

"Because. It's posher."

Tot got down from her chair and stood at the door that led to the front room. "Can I look in here again?"

"Alright." Stacey handed her the invitation and opened the front room door. The curtains were drawn back and pale-yellow strike flyers covered every inch of glass. The thin afternoon light filtered through the paper and cast a lemon haze over the room. For the two girls, it had the effect of transforming the room with its threadbare carpet and cheap furniture into a golden cave filled with soft light.

"Won't your mum mind having to make tea for everyone in the dark?" Tot asked. "Mine would."

"No. Mum says we all need to pull together. Like in the blitz."

"And your dad can make those lights come on?"

"My dad can make anything."

* * * * *

It was now dark inside the Wright's front room. The drizzle of the afternoon had given way to a deluge of rain that seemed set in for the remainder of the day. The yellow posters with their back-to-front words no longer cast the room in a golden glow. Now, the only light came from the hissing gas fire and the forty-watt standard lamp behind her father's chair.

Her father had a thing about lights. For as long as she could remember, he had hounded them all about turning them off and saving electricity. But since the miners went on strike, he'd run around telling everyone he met to switch all their lights on. He told the delivery men, the rent man, the man in the sweet shop. Everyone he met. He said it was to do with running down the National Grid. But when she went round the house turning all their lights on, he told her to switch them back off again. "Just the rich bastards, Stace," he'd told her. "Them who can afford it."

She sat on the worn settee and concentrated on her mother's slippers. Looking up would mean meeting her gaze, which would confirm that what had seemed a good idea this morning had now turned into a very bad idea.

"So, tell me again, Stacey," her mother said. "What made you think it would be a good idea to invite the Thompsons over for their tea tonight?"

She wondered how long she could get away without justifying the invitations and continued to watch her mother's feet. The pink fun-fur slippers had holes cut out so her beautiful bunions could poke through. Stacey had a ritual of checking her own feet each night for telltale bumps. There was nothing yet, but there was time. After all, her mother was at least forty.

"Ted, she's only gone and invited the Thompsons from number seventeen over for tea tonight." Her father sat facing away from them in his chair next to the bookcase. He was reading *The Socialist Worker* and making his way steadily through a bowl of winkles. She could see their shiny little shells heaped up in the bowl on the arm of the chair. She didn't know how he could stand to put snails in his mouth, even if they did come from the sea and not their back garden.

Her mother continued. "I mean, the O'Flannerys I could understand," she said, "but Mr. and Mrs. High-And-Mighty Thompson?"

Stacey watched her father's prized winkle pin flash as his hand moved from the bowl, then back to his mouth. She wished he would say something rather than just sitting there spearing snails and reading his paper.

Her mother turned back to Stacey. "What was going on in that head of yours? There's nothing in the fridge, we're low on bread, and the electric's due to go off at seven."

Stacey tried her best. "There's chocolate cake. . . ."

"The cake is for the Residents' meeting tomorrow night! Now I'll have to make another one and I'm all out of cocoa. Ted, speak to her."

Her father was a big man, and the hands that held the paper and winkling pin were clean, yet stained from years of printing ink and hard work. He said nothing, merely turned the page, took another winkle from the bowl, and stretched his legs out. He rested his feet on the bank of car batteries that sat against the base of the bookcases like oversized Lego bricks. His toes caressed the corners of the batteries. This was his *pièce de résistance*, his pride and joy. The batteries were connected to two stainless steel spotlights that hung from each corner of the bookcase like silver cupcakes.

Her mother shook her head and sat down on the sofa. "Come on. Just one good reason. That's all I want." She put her hand underneath Stacey's chin and tilted her face. "Just one good reason."

She bit her lip. "Dad said—"

"Dad said to invite them over? Ted?"

"No. Dad said everyone had to know about the miners and their strike and the ponies, and Mrs. Thompson doesn't because she won't let Tot put posters in their window—"

"You see what you've done to the child, Ted," her mother said. "God save us all from bloody politics."

Stacey sniffed, ". . . and because Daddy made the lights work, and Tot didn't believe me, and . . . and I said that you said it was like in the Blitz and that we all had to be good neighbours. So, I thought they could come round for their tea." She felt the tears begin to sting behind her eyes and a lump the size of the Bishop's Croft community centre gathered at the back of her throat. "Tot's dad plays the trumpet."

"Well, I suppose that makes it all right then! We'll all have a bit of a sing-song! What are you going to play, Ted? The Didgerie-bloody-doo!" Her mother stood up, cheeks flushed and plump hands on hips. "What are we going to do with you, Stacey Wright?" she said. "I said, what are we going to do with her, Ted?"

Her father folded the paper in half and, placing the bowl on the floor next to his chair, turned round to face his wife and youngest daughter. His lips were twisted into a maniacal grin and his face was covered with the small black trap doors he'd prised from each of his Sunday winkles. He stood up and, with his arms raised above his head, lurched towards the sofa groaning, "WINKLE MAN DOESN'T DO THE DID-GERIDOO! ARGHHH!"

Her mother sniffed and straightened the ties on her apron. "You're both as bad as each other," she said, heading out to the kitchen in search of something other than chocolate cake with which to feed the Thompsons. Stacey buried her face in a cushion as her father tickled her and winkle lids rained down onto the sofa.

* * * * *

Stacey's father, minus winkle lids, sat in the chair under the emergency spotlights. One spot was trained on the sofa on which sat the two mothers. They were both in their forties, but there the similarity ended. Stacey's mother had changed out of her housecoat into a balding, yellow velour tracksuit that clung to each hummock and hill of her body. She had caught her long hair up in a yellow plastic bobbler. Tot's mother wore an African-print kaftan and mock-croc high-heeled sandals. Her toenails were the colour of seashells. Each time she lifted her teacup, a clatter of silver bangles jangled around her thin forearms.

The other spotlight illuminated the rug in front of the gas fire where Stacey and Tot sat leafing through a copy of the Kay's catalogue.

Stacey's mother coughed to break the brittle silence. "Stacey, dear, pass Mr. Thompson another salmon sandwich." Stacey leant forward and took the plate from the tile-topped coffee table and offered it to Mr. Thompson, who was sitting in a chair identical to her father's on the opposite side of the fireplace.

"Well, thank you, Mrs. Wright. Maybe just another one." He took a sandwich and wedged it onto his plate against the large slice of chocolate cake and cubes of cheese and pineapple speared on a cocktail stick. His chubby face was shadowy under the clinical glare of the spotlights.

Stacey set the plate on the table and sat back down next to Tot on the rug. They took turns picking their favourite thing from each catalogue page. She selected Farrah Fawcett's red lycra jumpsuit, and Tot opted for her silver platform boots.

Mr. Thompson slid the speared cheese and pineapple from the cocktail stick with his teeth and used it to point at the spotlights. "Fine get-up, Mr. Wright. Your emergency lights are just the ticket." Her father nodded, but said nothing. Mr. Thompson continued. "How long do you think the miners will be out this time?"

Her father shrugged his shoulders. "As long as it takes, Mr. Thompson. As long as it takes."

The two women sat at either end of the sofa. On the cushion between them lay the hand-coloured invitation. Mrs. Thompson had eaten her sandwich, and her plate was empty.

Mrs. Wright pulled at the tight legs of her tracksuit. "More tea? Some cake, perhaps?" she said.

"No, thank you." Mrs. Thompson put her plate down on the floor by the side of the sofa. She crossed her legs and leaned towards Mr. Wright. "I just hope they realise they can't hold the country to ransom."

Stacey's father tapped his fingers on the *The Socialist Worker* that lay open on the hearth. "Some people don't see it that way, Mrs. Thompson." He smiled all the time he spoke. Both Stacey and her mother knew that was a bad sign. When Mr. Wright smiled and talked politics, he intended to win. "When they marched on the House of Commons last week, the paper says the crowd strung out for three miles."

"No doubt padded with football hooligans and anarchists," she replied, dabbing at her mouth with a small linen handkerchief.

"Not padded," he replied. "Supported by over seventy-five percent of the thinking public, isn't that right, Pat?"

Stacey's mother looked from Mrs. Thompson to her husband and back again. "Ted, I don't think this is really the time or place to be getting into politics. Let's leave the miners and the strike for another day." She picked up the invitation. "Did you colour this in, dear?" she said to Tot.

Tot looked up from the Kay's catalogue and nodded.

"It's very good," she said. "Is this one of the little ponies you ride at the weekend?"

Tot shook her head. "No. It's a pit pony that hasn't had anything to eat for seven weeks because all the miners have to walk around with big signs and can't afford to buy it any hay or carrots or anything. It's probably dead by now." She went back to the catalogue and selected an exercise bike complete with milometer.

Mrs. Wright looked uncomfortable and Mrs. Thompson looked at her watch. "Gosh," she said. "Is that the time? I'm so sorry, but we're going to have to be going. Have to pick up our Dorothy from Am-Dram."

Stacey's mother looked puzzled. "Am-Dram?" she asked.

"Amateur Dramatics, Mrs. Wright." She stood up and brushed crumbs off her kaftan onto the carpet. "She's playing Persephone, you know. And she's only fourteen."

"Oh, it's Patricia. Please call me Patricia. What a shame you have to run off so early."

"Well, maybe another time. Are you coming, Donald?" She stared at her husband, a pink-lacquered nail rapping on the glass of her wristwatch.

He took a bite from a salmon sandwich, then seemed to study Mr. Wright, who sat silent and smiling in his chair by the fire. "Nope," he said, cramming the rest of the sandwich triangle into his mouth. "You take the car and I'll see you later on. I want to talk to Mr. Wright about his emergency lighting system." She glared at him, then turned on her heel and disappeared into the gloom of the hallway. Stacey's mother hurried after her.

The front door slammed. Stacey watched her father smiling broadly in his chair. Mr. Thompson had stood up to investigate the spotlights when Mrs. Wright reappeared in the doorway with a teapot in her hand. "More tea, Donald?" she asked.

"How about a beer?" suggested Stacey's father. Mr. Thompson looked across to the smiling woman in the doorway, a brown teapot in her hands and her yellow tracksuit smeared with icing sugar and jam.

"You know," he said, "a beer would be great. Thank you, Mr. Wright. I really appreciate your hospitality."

"It's Ted, Donald. Call me Ted."

* * * * *

When her mother disappeared back to the kitchen, Stacey pulled Tot into the dark space behind the sofa.

"What are we doing?" asked Tot.

"We're hiding," Stacey whispered. "They say all the good stuff when they can't see you." She lay on her stomach in the cramped space between the sofa and the wall. She could only see shoes and ankles between the legs of the sofa.

"Are they going to play gin rummy now?" asked Tot, raising her head above the top of the cushion backs.

"Shhh!" She tugged at Tot's waistband and hauled her back down. "No, they're going to drink beer."

"My dad doesn't drink beer. Mum says it's common."

"What does he drink then?"

"Gin and tonic. With a bit of lemon in it."

"Gosh," Stacey said. "Real lemon?"

"Yeah."

* * * * *

"So, Ted, you're all in favour of the strike, then." Stacey saw Mr. Thompson's empty beer bottle join three others on the carpet next to his chair.

"I'm in favour of a fair day's pay for a fair day's work. And I think they do a fair day, don't you, Don?"

She heard Mr. Thompson fumble with another bottle and the bottle opener. "I suppose so. But even so, we can't all have lights like you've got here. I mean, you're a practical man. And these power cuts are driving my wife barmy."

"I can see they might."

Mr. Thompson dropped the bottle opener with a clang onto the hearth. "Whoops a daisy!" he said. "This homebrew's strong, Ted!"

"Yes, it can certainly creep up on you . . . if you're not used to it. Here, let me do that for you."

"Many thanks, old man." He slipped his shoes off, and Stacey could see his feet in their patterned socks stretched out in front of the fire. She watched him wiggle his toes.

Tot had fallen asleep and began to snore. Stacey gently pinched her nose like she'd seen her mother do when her dad's snoring got too loud. Tot gulped once or twice and then fell back into a silent sleep. Stacey went back to watching Mr. Thompson, who was still wiggling his snazzy toes.

"Hmm," he said, "beer, eh? A man's drink, wouldn't you say, Ted?"

"Oh, yes. Definitely a man's drink."

"Of course, Elaine doesn't like to see a man drinking beer. She says it's common." Mr. Thompson dropped a peeled label onto the floor. It stuck to his foot. "I hope you don't mind me saying this, Ted, but I have to say . . . I envy you, old man."

"Why should I mind?"

Mr. Thompson held his feet up to the fire. "Because you might not have a lot, Ted. But what's yours is yours. Lovely lady wife, crate of beer in the larder, happy as a sand boy, right?" His words began to slur. "I know what everyone thinks about me . . . all you Stanley Close men. 'The High and Mighty Thompsons at number seventeen.' Ideas above their station' and all that. But it's not me, you see. It's Elaine. Always pushing for something else. New curtains, new carpet. Moving up, moving out. You?

You're the king of your own modest little three-bedroom castle, right Ted?"

"That's right."

"But me, I'm just . . . I'm just the Jack. No . . . no, I'm not even the Jack. I'm the Ten of Hearts. Or maybe the Joker. That's it! I'm the trumpet-playing Joker!"

"Have another beer, Don."

"Thanks, Ted. You know, bugger Elaine! I'm going to start drinking beer from now on. And she can forget the glass. Straight from the bottle! Bugger 'em all!" Stacey heard him successfully uncap a beer. The lid flew across the room and landed on Tot's chest. She didn't wake up.

"You wouldn't see a miner drinking gin and tonic now, would you, Ted?"

"Probably not, Don. Probably not."

Donald appeared to slip a little lower in his seat, the turn-ups of his suit trousers coming into Stacey's view. "Oh, no," he said. "I don't see a miner with a gin and tonic in his hand. No siree. Ha!" he snorted. "Ha! Tell you what, eh, Ted. Wouldn't go down well in the old Wheel Tappers' and Shunters' Club, would it?"

"What's that, Don?"

"You know, some grimy old miner standing at the bar with a flat cap in one hand and a whippet on baler twine in the other—'I say, my man. Mine's a gin and tonic—ice and a slice, 'eh, what?'" He laughed and put the bottle down on the carpet next to the sofa. "Jesus, your lights are the business, Ted. Our bloody house is as dark as the black hole of Calcutta. Just me and Elaine on the sofa with a torch three nights a week. Bloody country's going to the dogs, eh?" Her father didn't answer. "So what's your solution, Ted? What's your advice to the nation?"

Before he could answer, the front room main lights came back on. Her father reached down to the bookcase and disconnected the wires from the car batteries. Donald stood up, knocking over the half-empty bottle of beer. A puddle of froth bubbled on the hearth.

"Support the men from the coalface," her father said. "Support them and switch all your lights on, Don. Leave your lights on and run down the National Grid. That's what you should do."

"All the lights? Even in rooms I'm not using?"

"All the lights, Don."

"Consider it done. Our place'll be shining like Crystal Palace. A beacon for the boys on the coalface!"

Suddenly, the sofa shifted forward and Stacey looked up to see her father smiling down at her. He picked up Tot in his arms.

"Here's your littlest," he said, handing over the sleeping girl to Mr. Thompson. Tot still wore Dorothy's green platform shoes. They hung from her feet like bright leaves. Her hand was furled tight as a fiddlehead around a shiny metal bottle top. Stacey stood up and sleepily grabbed her father's hand. He ruffled her hair.

Mr. Thompson placed a wet kiss on Tot's forehead. "Did you know I played the trumpet, Ted?"

Her father patted him on the shoulder. "You go home, Don," he said, "and turn all those lights on."

"Right-o, Ted. That's what I'll do. As bright as bloody Crystal Palace." He weaved gently down the hallway and out the front door, clutching Tot to his chest.

"Don't forget, now," called her father. "Switch all those lights on."

"Up the miners!" called Mr. Thompson.

Stacey and her father stood on the front door step and watched him head back across the grass towards his house. When he reached his front garden, illuminated by the Victorian replica gaslight, they stepped back into the hallway. Her father shut the door and walked across to the front room to turn off the lights.

"Remember, Stace, my love," he said. "Just the rich bastards." He took her hand again, turned off the hall light, and the pair of them made their way carefully up the stairs to bed.

Our mum does the washing on Saturday mornings. She washes, my sister hangs it out, and we all bring it back indoors when it's dry. Today, it froze, and I carried our mum and dad's bottom sheet up the alley like a piece of hardboard. I had to crack it in the middle to get it through the back door.

My special job is sorting the knickers, socks, and nighties.

I've got seven pairs of socks and seven pairs of knickers. Knickers are pairs, because you can get a pair of legs in them. If you only had one leg, like Keesal's Dad, they'd still be a pair. Unless you had a sewing machine and could stitch up a leg. Then it'd be "a" knicker. Or "a" pant.

Me and Dorothy have got one nightie each, but our Mum's got two. One blue one like mine with elastic around the collar and cuffs, and one red and black Baby Doll. It's got slippy knickers that match.

It's not in the washing basket every week. I think she only wears it for Best.

The Gongoozler

✺

Tot marvelled that a ten-by-twelve shed could contain so much stuff. As well as storing the deckchairs and lawn-mower, it was home to two forgotten sacks of bulbs, seed trays, potting compost, a boxed shell collection that had belonged to her father, empty jam jars, twenty-four bottles of flexo-graphic ink in a host of colours, a chest of drawers containing knobs, handles, screws and nails, and a painting of a blue lady Uncle Ernie had given them for Christmas last year. It was also home to Tot's fishing nets, which were proving hard to find. She moved the deck chairs, each one unfolding like an ungainly giraffe. Everything seemed to be wrapped in web, and Tot didn't get along with spiders. She spotted the nets' bamboo handles and dragged them out from behind the burlap sacks of spring bulbs. They were smashers. Four-foot handles with pink nylon nets.

"I've found them! We can have one each." She stepped out of the shed into the eye-squinting April morning. Keesal Patel sat peering into a bucket by the back door step. The bucket was full of sticklebacks and pondweed, each fish a tawny silver, almost transparent. He trailed one brown finger in the water, trying to touch their smooth, slick sides. Tot hunkered down next to him.

"Do they have sticklebacks in India?" she asked.

"I don't know!" he said. "I never lived in India."

She sprinkled dried fish food on the surface of the water. The fish clustered around the pellets, dragged them below and then released them with a leisurely pop.

"There's forty-two in there. Look," she said, pointing to the five-bar gates drawn on the bucket's side. "Just seven more to go, and my Dad'll come back." She picked up two large jam jars by the string loops around their necks. "Come on then, if you're coming! Don't forget the sandwiches."

* * * * *

The Grand Union canal cut through the county, and when it encountered the village of Bishop's Croft, it navigated the humps and valleys with a series of locks. The longest flight started above the yard that flanked Roker's Ink Factory, and this was the spot Tot chose for the morning's fishing.

The water's surface was smooth and glassy and reflected the willows that hung over the water, their fresh green branches trailing like hair in a basin. A fringe of yellow foam collected towards the other bank, effluent from the factory. Rainbow metal drums, bright as Liquorice Allsorts, were stacked two high in the yard. Each contained the resins and chemicals required for the inks her dad used to make. Inks like Cobalt Blue and Process Black for I.P.C. Newspapers and Carmine Red 167 for Mother's Pride, their bread bag signature colour. He'd told her about the toffee resins that arrived from Africa. Huge shipments, folded like miles of bed sheets, chipped and stored in green barrels. He'd scared her with stories of exotic spiders in resin deliveries from Nigeria and of explosions in the Dispersement Building, a tin hut where two men shovelled nitrous cellulose, as soft as soap flakes, into a grinder.

The shiny hues of the containers clashed with a gaudy barge that nosed its way inexpertly towards the uppermost lock. The narrow boat, *The Gongoozler*, was a holiday hire from Palmerstone Boats in Northampton. An elderly man with a peaked cap stood at the tiller shouting directions to his heavy wife, who struggled to open the gates with a long lock key.

Tot waited until the barge was in the lock and the gates had shut before dipping both jam jars in the water. They filled with noisy glugs, and murky water swirled inside. She pulled out most of the pond weed, leaving one frilly spiral in each, and set each jar back on the towpath. She sat back next to Keesal on the bench by the railway bridge that spanned the canal. The boat had to go through the lock and pass under the bridge before the fish would return from the safety of the willow-fringed water.

"My dad was going to take us on a canal boat for our holidays," she said, "but mum wanted to go to Benidorm. That's in Spain."

"I know where it is. What was it like?"

"We didn't go."

"Why not?"

Tot picked up one of the nets and peered inside the nylon mesh to check that the seam was on the outside. If you caught a stickleback and the seam was on the inside, you could rip its belly open. She'd done that last Saturday and had to catch another one. Catching seven was difficult, but eight sticklebacks could take all day.

"Why didn't you go?" Keesal asked again, taking a foil parcel of sandwiches and a plastic bottle filled with orange squash from a Sainsbury's carrier bag.

"Because my dad left."

"Where did he go?"

"America. To play the trumpet. But he's coming back."

"When?"

"I don't know. Maybe next week. Or in May. It's a deal I made with God."

"What deal?"

Tot looked up at Keesal. "Can I come to your house for tea?"
He scuffed the toe of his plimsoll in the gravel around the
bench. "I'm not allowed to have anyone round."

"Aw, go on. Or else I won't tell you about the deal."

"If you don't tell me, you can't have any of my sandwiches."
Keesal picked up the foil parcel and put it down on the far side
of the bench.

"Don't want your stinky curry sandwiches anyway," Tot
said. "And if you don't let me have one, you can't have a net."
Tot waved to the elderly couple, who had managed to navigate
the lock and were now inching their way through the narrow
bridge. The fat woman waved back.

Keesal wiped his nose on his sleeve and mumbled.

"What did you say?" Tot asked.

"I said they're not curry." He opened the parcel, took out a
sandwich, and peeled back the top slice of bread. Tot leant forward to sniff the brown filling and Keesal dabbed it on her nose.

"Eugh! I don't like curry!" said Tot.

"S'not curry. Lick it."

Tot rubbed her nose with her finger and licked it clean.
"Mmmm. Chocolate spread!" she said. "I didn't think Indians
would like chocolate spread."

Keesal chewed and nodded. "Everyone likes chocolate
spread. It's . . . universal—like presents . . . or clean sheets."

"Or new socks," Tot said.

He nodded. "All right, I'll ask my mum if you can come
round for your tea. Now, what deal?"

"I did a deal with God that if I catch seven sticklebacks for
seven Saturdays, he wouldn't let my dad go to America."

"But you said he'd gone."

"He went before we were ready. I'd only got seven, so it
didn't work. We hadn't ironed out all the details."

The Gongoozler had made it safely out from below the
bridge and the lady jumped from the towpath back onto the
barge's narrow walkway. "Come on, let's fish," Tot said.

She sat on the edge of the towpath and dipped her net
in the water. Keesal sat down beside her. "He's coming back

though," she said. "God wouldn't welsh on a deal, would he?" She looked across at the boy. "Do they have God in India, too?" He took a bite from his sandwich. "I think so. What are you going to do with the fish? Let them go?" She trailed the net over the surface of the dark water. "Nah. Sacrifice them. Squish 'em with a house brick. You have to, for God. In Benidorm, they throw goats out of belfries. Did you know that?"

"What's a belfry?"

"Dunno, but they're high."

Tot saw a fat, brown stickleback nosing the opposite bank just below the surface. She stretched out on her front on the towpath. "Hold my legs!" she said and edged the fishing net out across the water. It didn't quite reach, but that didn't matter. Keesal held onto her legs while she waited. "You can't chase a fish," she whispered. "You have to decide where he wants to go, and then wait for him." She held the net steady until the fish glided backwards an inch, turned once, and then swam into the pink nylon mesh. She scooped the net from the water, gently palmed the fish, and dropped it into her jam jar. Six more to go.

* * * * *

They had eaten half the sandwiches and finished off the orange squash. Keesal hadn't proved himself to be a very good fisherman and his jar was home to one solitary minnow no bigger than a little finger. But they fished in companionable silence, the only noise the slap of the water against the sides of the canal and the low hum of traffic on the motorway.

Keesal scratched the side of his foot with the handle of his fishing net. "Tot," he said. "Can I ask you something?"

"Yeah."

"You won't be angry?"

"No. What?"

"Are you mental?"

"'Course I'm not mental! Why?"

"My mum said you were."

Tot stared at Keesal. "Why?"

"Because you get fits. We had an auntie in Calcutta who had fits. She was a loonie."

Tot sat quietly for a second or two and then slapped at the water's surface with her net, scaring a group of moorhens that were heading for the shadow of the bridge. "You tell your mum I'm not mental. Seamus O'Flannery is mental. I just get fits sometimes. All right?"

Keesal nodded. "What happens if you get a fit?"

"What, like now?"

"Yeah."

She lifted her net out and rested it on the towpath. "Well, I won't because I took my tablet with my Ready-Brek, and I've got another one here for dinnertime." She pulled a plastic bottle from her pocket, rattled it, and placed it on the ground next to the glass jar of fish.

"Yeah, but if you did. What happens?"

"It tastes like I'm sucking pennies and then the sound goes up and down and sometimes I fall over. I don't really know what else."

"Is that it?"

"Sometimes I wee my pants. Not every time though."

"Ergh!"

"It's not my fault. It's the fits."

"I know," he said. "I'm just kidding." He balled up the foil and threw it across the pathway into the litter bin by the bench. "What would I have to do? I mean, if you did have one."

"You're meant to get my mum, but we're too far away."

"So what would I have to do?" he asked again.

"Dad says you should put a pencil in my mouth, so I don't bite my tongue off, but that's like with a big fit, and I've not had one of those for ages."

"But I haven't got a pencil. I've only got a pen and it's my best one."

Tot looked around. "You could use the handle of my fishing rod. But check there's no fish in the net first."

"What's in your tablets?" Keesal asked.

"Chemical horses. Like stallions made out of medicine."

"My mum said—"

"I don't CARE what your mum said. It's your mum what's mental."

The moorhens recovered their composure, and the group of five ducklings, headed by their mother, floated past below the bridge.

"What did your mum say?" Tot asked.

"My mum said it's an invasion of the heart."

"What is?"

"Epilepsy."

"That's stupid. Do they take tablets in India?"

"No. Mum said they boil rice in milk and then feed it to a pig."

"What? Any pig or a special pig?"

"I don't know. But then they kill the pig and stick it in a big oven. Then you pull out its stomach and mix it with wine and drink it."

"Ugh!"

"Or you can mix up special herbs with juice made from cow pooh."

Tot shook her head. "They don't like epileptics in India, do they?"

"Some people do yoga."

"What's that? Is it like yoghurt? My mum eats yoghurt. Yoghurt with hazelnuts."

"No, it's like an exercise where you sit down with your legs crossed and bend about a lot. You can do it to Indian music if you want."

"I think I'll stick with the tablets," Tot said. "What's an invasion?"

Then in the distance came the sound of a train. It whistled once, a low moan, and then again. This time, a long shrill note. Tot scrambled backwards and pressed her ear to the brickwork of the bridge. It was still damp and clammy from the morning's frost. She rubbed her ear. "You can feel the train coming through the bricks," she said.

Keesal rested his net on the towpath and stooped down under the arch of the bridge next to her, his ear to the brickwork.

"You can kiss me if you want." Tot said. He didn't answer. She pulled the sleeve of his parka. "Not a real one. Just a practice." She closed her eyes and pursed her lips, her ear still against the brickwork. He gave her a glancing, clumsy kiss, and she licked her lips. They tasted of chocolate and toothpaste. Keesal darted out from underneath the bridge back into the sunlight. She watched him scramble up the embankment. "Where are you going?" she called.

"I want to get its number."

She crawled up the embankment after him, the grass staining her bare knees. Keesal stood at the top of the ridge, shielding his eyes, and watched the distant train rocking down the tracks towards them. She stood at his side. The wind was strong and ruffled the fur lining of his parka hood and filled her skirt with little puffs of wind. "Do they have trains in Calcutta?" she asked.

"Oh Tot, of course they do! It's not all elephants and curry." He pulled a notepad and a pen from his pocket. The tracks began to hum a low, even tune.

"What date is it?" he asked.

"April 26th, 1972."

He opened the notepad. "I know the year, silly!" he said and wrote the date at the top of the page

"Are Indian trains like our trains?" she asked.

"I don't know," he said. "I've only been there once, and I was just a baby."

"How much of a baby?"

"About three."

"You must remember something," she said. "I remember having my photo taken when I was three, and my mum pricked me with a big pin."

"You do not!"

"I do!" She sat down on the grassy bank. In the distance, the train was growing from a small speck on the horizon to something the size of an eraser on the end of a pencil.

Keesal sat down next to her. "I remember the smell," he said.

"What was it like?"

"It smelt like roads on a really hot day. Like when the tarmac melts. And there was a woman cooking meatballs on the platform. My dad bought some and gave me one. It was horrible. It tasted like Spam. And the platform was kind of juddering as the train came in. But that might have been my Dad."

"What did the train look like?"

"I don't remember. But I do remember I was wearing sandals with blue donkeys on the toes."

"You remember your sandals but not the train? That's stupid."

"It's what I remember. You asked."

The train was bigger now. It was the size of her fingernail and growing all the time. The song from the steel tracks had grown louder and hummed at their feet. She could feel the vibration through the long bone in her chest. She lay back on the grassy rise just two or three feet from the track. "Lay down," she said.

"I want to get the number."

"You can still get the number. Lay here." She patted the grass next to her, then held out her hand.

He lay down, his body as stiff as a stair rod, with his notepad in one hand and Tot's fingers in the other. The train came nearer. The grass was long and grew up around them. She could feel the last of the morning dew. It seeped cold through her skirt, but her hand was warm in Keesal's. The train was nearly on them now. Keesal sat up for a second, then lay back down in the grass as the train thundered through. The air was thick and dark with the giant smell of diesel and old oil. The wind raced across them, lifting her skirt and fanning her orange curls out through the grass. Keesal's parka filled with air and all around them, the grass pressed down flat against the ground.

Then the train was rushing past them down the line towards London, and the smell of diesel hung for a moment and was then sucked up behind the carriages. The grass bobbed back up and the sun broke over the ink factory making the barrels twinkle and the little *Gongoozler* shine as it bumped through the locks further down the valley. Tot and Keesal lay quietly in the grass.

"Did you get the number?" she asked, feeling his damp fingers around her own.

"Yeah," he said.

She knew there was no way he could have made out the number on the train. It was going too fast. "Aren't you going to write it in the book?" she said.

"I need my hand back."

She let go of his hand and sat up, smoothing her skirt back down over her green-stained knees. Keesal sat up too, scribbled in his book, and then slid the pen behind his ear.

She grabbed the book from his grasp and held it above her head. "Liar! Liar! Pants on fire! You didn't get the number. Not even Batman could have got that number! Not even the Joker!"

"Give it back!"

"Come and get it!" She ran back down the embankment and along the towpath. Keesal followed and tried to grab the book, but she kept dodging around the lock gates, reading the pages as she went. It was full of numbers, but in the back, there was writing. There was a list of boy's names and dates and then, in the second from last column, Keesal had written things like "leg and shirt" or "mouth." This wasn't to do with trains.

Keesal grabbed the notepad back and retreated to the bench by the bridge. He took another sandwich from the foil parcel. Tot sat down next to him and took one as well. She pinched it flat between her fingers, then licked the butter and chocolate spread that squidged out from the sides.

"What's in the back of the book?" she said, taking a bite from the flattened sandwich.

"Just stuff."

"What kind of stuff?" she asked.

"Stuff. You know."

The book lay on the bench between them. She picked it up and turned to the back to read the last entry. "'Friday 25th April." She turned to Keesal. "That's yesterday." He nodded. She went back to the book. "'Friday 25th April. Nigel Deepens. Leg and Shirt'. What does that mean?" Keesal was silent. "What's the last column for?" she asked. The boy said nothing. "Come on," she said. "I told you about the fish and God. What does it mean?"

He stood and picked up his net. "Let's fish," he said and sat down on the towpath. She picked up the other net and sat next to him. "Come on. If we're proper friends, you have to tell me. It's the rules."

He trailed the net backwards and forwards. A water rat surfaced on the bank opposite and watched them for a moment before bobbing back down and swimming towards the willows, a fluid arrow through the water.

He sank the net deeper. "On Friday, by the community centre, Nigel Deepens beat me up." He pulled up his trouser leg to reveal a purple bruise on his shin and a jagged, newly scabbed gash on his knee. "He grabbed me by the tie and ripped my shirt." He rolled his trouser leg back down. "On Thursday, it was Michael O'Flannery, and he spat in my mouth."

Tot bit her lip. "What's the last column for?"

He lifted the net from the water and pulled it back towards him. Inside, in amongst the pondweed, flipped a tea-coloured stickleback. He wet his hand and gently cupped the fish, then dropped it into his jam jar. "That's two, anyway," he said.

"What's the last column for?"

"I'm going to tick it . . . when they stop." He dipped the net back in the water.

"Why do they beat you up?"

"Because I'm a Paki. Because I'm new. I don't know." He picked up the jar and watched the fish circle around the glass. "Do you think the fish thing would work for me?"

"How do you mean?" Tot said.

"Stop them. Stop them picking on me."

"It might do. Goats'd be better."

"Are there any goats in Bishop's Croft?"

"Nope. No belfries either," Tot said.

Water droplets fell in a steady stream from the underside of the railway bridge and onto the water, the ripples widening smoothly until the dark circles touched both sides of the narrow waterway. The water's surface reflected the slanting sun back onto the underside of the bridge, bubbles of white light dancing on the wet, blackened bricks.

"The fish didn't stop your dad from going," Keesal said.

"No, but they might bring him back."

"God should have stopped him going."

She was silent because inside she knew he was right.

"I could sacrifice them to Indra." Keesal peered into his net again, but it was empty.

"Who's Indra?"

"Indra's the god of thunder and rain. He's a great warrior, and he's got a big nose."

"He might be alright then. Does he like fish?" Tot leant back against the bridge.

Keesal dipped the net back into the water. "I don't know. He's got a big sword and a seashell. Oh, and in the picture in our kitchen, he's got a rope in one hand and there's a rainbow that comes out of one of his ears and disappears in the other."

"Do people pray to him?"

"Yeah, and they sacrifice animals. Slit their throats and stuff. Do you think the fish might work?"

Tot picked up her jar. She'd caught six sticklebacks, and they bumped into each other, nosing through the pondweed. A drop of cold wet rain fell on her cheek and the surface of the canal by the lock gates pocked and pooled with rain drops. She leaned across and emptied her six fish into Keesal's jar and handed him her fishing net.

"Come on," she said, standing up and brushing the dirt from the backs of her socks. "If we leg it, we might make it home before the storm starts."

Tot ran past the locks and out of the gate that led onto the main road back up to the housing estate. Keesal followed on behind her, one small hand stretched across the neck of his jam jar, the other tight around both fishing nets. He pushed the gate shut behind them with his foot, and they ran for the cover of the nearby overpass, Keesal slopping water onto the pale pavement slabs as he ran. Fat drops of rain quickly obliterated the dark patches of spilt canal water, and then the heavens opened, a deluge coursing down the gutters and leaving the pavement slick and shiny. From the shelter of the overpass, Tot and Keesal watched a second Palmerstone canal boat nudge into the open lock by the bridge and a woman in a plastic cagoule and Wellingtons struggle to push back the lock gate. The shrill whistle of another train coming down the line accompanied the stuttering pop of the boat's puttering engine.

SUMMER 1972

There's Stealing and Choiring and Borrowing. Stealing is when you take something from someone, and you don't give it back. Like Curly Wurlies. Or Fruit Pastilles. If you're a Roman Catholic like Lilly and Michael, you'll go to hell and have your hands tied up with snakes, and your head'll keep exploding.

Choiring is when you take things no one will miss. My Dad used to choir little bottles of ink and rubber gloves from Rokers. He painted his fishing floats with the ink, and mum wears the gloves when she does the weeding. She won't wear them in the front garden though.

Borrowing is taking something for a little while and then putting it back. Like Dorothy's shoes. Or Seamus's trousers. Borrowing's just like sharing.

Trouble

❖

In the hallway, the plastic laundry basket sat piled high with damp clothes. The skies had foretold of rain that morning and sure enough, it had waited until the day's washing was nearly dry before pouring down.

Lilly draped each damp garment over the wooden clothes horse that straddled the bath and grappled with this idea of predestination. It will continue to rain, she thought. She will get married, there will be children, a bedroom suite on the never-never, a rent book. Downstairs, all the people she loved appeared to have accepted this idea that their lives were already mapped out. Forever. Her brother Seamus seemed content with his Lego bricks and the prognosis that he would probably never speak his name or make love to a girl. His twin Michael, although football crazy, didn't dream of a life as a centre forward for Manchester United. He had already begun to work weekends for their uncle's laundry business, and harboured a mumbled desire to one day be the boss.

Through the pebbled window, she watched her father sitting on a dining room chair underneath the carport at the end of the garden. He'd decided to teach himself watch repairs after he was laid off from the ink factory. The smooth concrete beneath his boots was always littered with brass cogs and tiny springs.

She wondered at their mute acceptance as she hung up the washing. Nylon cartoon underpants for her brothers, her father's baggy Y-fronts, her own flower-strewn panties, bought last summer from Tammy Girl. When she picked out her mother's underwear, still stiff and stained from too many years of womanhood, she realised. It wasn't a case of predestination. It was purely a matter of acceptance.

* * * * *

Most of the other kids in Lilly's class at Our Lady of the Holy Cross wore their front door keys on chains round their necks. The poorer kids wore theirs on lengths of string that started white and smooth at the beginning of term, but by the summer had became knotted and as grey as their tide-marked necks. But their mother wouldn't let them have keys. Instead, her brothers stayed behind at Our Lady of the Holy Cross; Michael had football practice until five, and Seamus contented himself sitting in the tin hut at the edge of the pitch and burrowing under the blue mats, medicine balls, and yellow cotton team vests. Lilly was allowed to come home to Stanley Close but had to stay at Dorothy Thompson's house for an hour after school until her mother got home from work.

Today had been the last day of school before the summer holidays. The 893 bus dropped her off at the community centre just as Dorothy appeared around the corner of Willowswitch Lane. Lilly watched Dorothy throw her bag down on the ornamental cobbles at the side of the post office and pull a regulation grey gabardine macintosh from her satchel. She shrugged it on and did up the buttons before joining Lilly on the wall outside the community centre.

"Aren't you hot in that, Dorothy Thompson?" Lilly asked. "I'd have thought you would have been baking!"

Dorothy shook her head and pulled open the top of the mac to reveal a non-regulation fuzzy pink jumper. "Chris met me at the church. Mum has a fit if I change out of my uniform on the bus. Goes on and on about how much it cost her."

Lilly thanked her lucky stars that Our Lady of the Cross merely fixated on Madonna Blue and insisted that boys and girls wear navy anything with white shirts. The grey and mauve that Dorothy had to put up with at the grammar in Treeverton was hateful.

"Come on," said Dorothy. "I'm starving."

On their walk across the Green, Lilly half listened to Dorothy moaning on and on about her boyfriend. She was thinking back to the time before Mr. Thompson left for America. Each afternoon, if he was on the early shift, they would hear him practicing the trumpet in the box room at the front of the house. Lilly loved the beautiful, brassy music that fell from the tiny window at the top of the Thompson house. On hot summer afternoons, it had to compete with the racket from the myriad transistor radios that blared from windowsills below open kitchen windows. The chart music sounded thin in comparison to the perfect bold jazziness that hovered out from Mr. Thompson's trumpet.

But at some point, he always seemed to hit a wrong note, and there would be a pause before he returned to the beginning of the tune and started again. Lilly wished she could have just heard one tune all the way through.

She followed Dorothy down the garden path, pausing to run her fingers over the hammered metal of the replica gaslight that stood to the side of the pathway.

The back door was unlocked, and they walked into the kitchen. The room looked like something from one of those glossy house magazines Lilly leafed through in the newsagents. There were dried flowers in baskets above the cottage-style kitchen cabinets and a wood stove in the corner, flanked on either side by two huge ceramic Siamese cats. The electric kettle and fondue set matched, each a riot of blue flowers on an egg-yolk background. Next to them were canisters full of coloured pasta, dried fruit and muesli, alongside a fruit bowl piled high with peaches and bananas. Up high above the units hung a portable television from a bracket.

Mrs. Thompson sat at the breakfast bar peeling potatoes and watching a television chef prepare a romantic dinner for two. She smiled at them both, kissed Dorothy on the cheek and pointed to a tray containing a plate of chocolate biscuits and two glasses of milk. She turned back to the television chef.

Lilly picked a biscuit from the plate and sipped her milk. She always felt she might learn something important here if she could just keep quiet long enough to hear it. She watched Mrs. Thompson's painted fingernail deftly pick an eye from a potato. She had brilliant scarlet nails. Dorothy rolled her eyes at her mother, finished her milk, and disappeared down the hallway. Lilly reluctantly followed her out of the kitchen and up the stairs.

* * * * *

Dorothy stood in front of the cheval mirror in her parents' bedroom. Lilly threw her school bag on the landing and sat on the padded ottoman that guarded the foot of the big double bed like an old, sleeping dog. The bed was covered with a crocheted afghan in a mess of colours. Red and blue squares clashed with pink and green. She imagined it in her own beige bedroom, saw it fighting with the old pink nylon curtains and winning. She buried her fingers in the quilt, losing them in the crocheted loops.

Dorothy hitched up the waistband of her skirt another turn and examined her legs in the mirror. Lilly thought she was getting fat. But she still had lovely legs. Ice-skater's legs. Brown in "American Tan" tights and as smooth as butter.

"Are your hands clean?" Dorothy said to the mirror.

Lilly snatched her fingers from the soft wool. Dorothy could be a pain in the arse at times.

"My grandma made that. She's made me one too out of

oddments . . . from all the things she's knitted me and Tot."
Dorothy abandoned the mirror and flopped down across the
bed. "What does your grandma do?"

Lilly picked at a button on the velvet upholstery. "She's in a
home."

Dorothy sighed and checked her tights for runs. "We're
going to get a nurse when grandma gets decrep . . . when she
gets old. Like when she can't go to the toilet anymore. Mum
says it's un-humane to put people in homes. It's what poor
people do." She sat up and scooted round on the bed until her
face was level with Lilly's. "She says it's very, very vulgar."

She knew that it was time to go. Dorothy was in another
shitty mood and there was no point staying. Anyway, it had to
be five-thirty by now and her mother and the boys would be
home. Lilly stood up, smoothing the creases from the front of
her school skirt. "I've got to go now. It's time for my tea."

"Tea? Don't you mean dinner?"

The creases refused to budge from the pleated grey skirt.
She caught a glimpse of herself in Dorothy's mirror. Her school
skirt was scrunched up, exposing her skinny white legs. Too
much skin.

"Yeah," she said. "Dinner."

* * * * *

Lilly was alternately proud and ashamed of her mother.
Proud because she was a stylist at André's, and therefore had
pretty hair each week, but ashamed because her mother had
to work full-time. But as Lilly's mother insisted on reminding
them, since Mr. O'Flannery had lost his job, it was her money
that floated the family, put bread on the table and shoes on
their feet.

Every morning before her mother left the house, Lilly
watched her tie a chiffon scarf the colour of old ladies' veins
carefully around her lacquered blonde hair and check herself
in the yellow plastic mirror that hung above the kitchen sink.

On a school day, they all walked together to the bus stop on Willowswitch Lane and waited for the bus that would take her and her brothers to Our Lady and her mother to the salon. But today was the first day of the school holidays, and the routine was broken. She watched her mother check her make-up once more in the mirror.

"Now, listen up, all of you," her mother said. "You're on best behaviour, you hear?" She tied the scarf in a tight bow under her plump chin. "Don't be bothering your father. He's got the garden to dig and doesn't need to be running after you lot." She picked up a thermos flask of tea from the kitchen worktop. "Any shenanigans, and it'll be off to your granddad's for the rest of the holidays."

Lilly and her brothers were immediately silent at the breakfast table.

"Michael, Seamus," her mother said, "listen to your sister. She's in charge."

Michael wailed. "Why's she always in charge?" He kicked Lilly under the table.

"Because she's fourteen, and you're twelve. That's all you need to know!"

"When do I get to be in charge?" he asked.

"When you're older than your sister, then you'll be the man. Now think on and be good." She made Lilly and the boys promise not to eat in the street or to leave the house in their pyjamas and slippers. After all, she told them from the back gate, she might have to work for a living, but she wouldn't have the neighbours thinking her family didn't know how to behave.

Lilly sat at the table playing with her breakfast—a Walls' pork sausage wrapped up in a slice of Mother's Pride. She was too old for Pig-in-a-Blanket. She hated Pig-in-a-Blanket. The sausage was always full of strange bouncy lumps, and the heat of the lard melted the butter on her bread, so it ran down her wrists and stained her dressing gown cuffs. Michael had left the table as soon as his mother clicked the back gate shut. She could hear the clatter of his football boots from the bedroom above, then the slap of a ball bouncing on the stairs, the occasional thud as he kicked it against the hall wall.

"I'm telling Mum!" she called out from her chair at the table. "You're not to play with that ball in the house. She said!"

Michael poked his sharp little face around the kitchen door. "Fuck off, Sticky Slapper," he snarled and disappeared back through the hallway, the bounce of the ball a steady beat on the floor.

His taunt made her throat ache. She threw the sausage sandwich at the kitchen door. "You're . . . vulgar, you are!" she screamed. "A bloody little vulgar pig!"

The front door slammed.

Seamus smeared his sausage across the tablecloth. Its plastic skin split, and he pressed minced pork and breadcrumbs through the bamboo slats of his placemat. She wedged her empty plate in the sink, along with the frying pan, mugs and spatula, and went upstairs to her bedroom.

On the foot of the bed was the Sainsbury's bag her mother had handed her the previous evening. Inside was a fluffy cream knitted tank top, a green Tonic skirt and a pair of Wellington boots. Mrs. Thompson had brought them round, her mother explained. They no longer fitted Dorothy, but she thought they might do for Lilly. She pulled out the tank top and hung it on a wooden hanger. She remembered Sadie Wright's wardrobe with three skirts and two shirts on one wire hanger. Lilly's mother said the best thing you could do with wire hangers was throw them away. She said a wire hanger was a sure sign of poverty.

She checked the label in the skirt. "Age 12-14. Warm Wash. Dry Flat." She shook her head. It would have to take its chance, she thought, like the rest of us.

The skirt hung from her bony hips and skimmed her knees. If she turned from side to side, the light from the window caught the skirt, changing its colour from slate grey to ivy. The skirt's shifting tones were the colour of stones in a river bed.

She draped her dressing gown over the end of the bed and reached back into the wardrobe for the tank top. She pulled the top down over her head and threaded her too-chubby arms through the tight armholes. She ran her hands across her breasts, feeling the jumper's rabbit softness beneath her palms. Her breasts felt like peaches, like the peaches they had for breakfast last year in Wales. They'd sat at a table set with a stiff white tablecloth and placemats on which five foxes ran from five sets of horses and snarling hounds. In the middle had been a white bowl brimming with peaches, each fruit fading from crayon purple to the palest yellow and covered in soft fuzz. She had never tasted peaches and ate four before her poached eggs arrived. She then spent the entire morning being sick into a plastic bucket in her parent's room. She remembered the press of the handle on her forehead and the rain crying down the casement windows. She remembered her mother being angry over a missed outing for holiday souvenirs.

Downstairs, Seamus was crying. Not wet crying, just that monotonous dry cry he did when he was bored or angry about something. Sighing, she shut the wardrobe door, and then trailed slowly down the stairs to the front room, humming to herself to drown out the sobbing that came from the kitchen.

She sat on the carpet with her back to the bay window, the orange floral curtains closed tightly to stop the furniture fading. Muted cries of "offside" sifted through the open half-lights, and the methodical drone of lawn mowers being pushed twelve feet up front lawns and twelve feet back down again made her sleepy. The sound reminded her of bees flying and feeding.

She pulled her mother's spherical make-up mirror from the cupboard under the television set and set it on the fire hearth. Her mother had mirrors in every room—the yellow plastic kitchen mirror; this one; the mirror inset into the cocktail bar in the dining room. The face in the mirror was round and soft, skin pink from too much weekend sunbathing on the old camp bed in the back garden. Her mouth was wide and distinct. Her lips dark red, the top a little fuller than the bottom. Her mother said they would get her into trouble. She swivelled the mirror down from her mouth: cream tank top, green skirt, no shoes.

She wondered about this trouble. She'd been there when her mother mentioned it to the host of aunts that came to visit.

They'd be sitting at the kitchen table shaking their heads, and they'd put down their teacups and turn their sad gaze on Lilly, as if she wasn't to be blamed, more pitied.

She turned the mirror to the magnify side and opened her lips, looking at the darkness at the back of her throat, lifting her tongue and watching the saliva catch behind her bottom teeth.

The sun beat on the back of her neck through the thick curtains. She combed her hair with outstretched fingers. It felt hot, like one of Mrs. Thompson's china stove cats. She put the mirror away in the cupboard and walked back into the kitchen, trailing her hand along the cool tiled walls. Her mother wouldn't be home until five o'clock.

There was a family-sized tin of tomato soup in the kitchen in a saucepan and one slice of Mother's Pride left in the bread bin. She was hungry, having missed out on breakfast. She opened the can and poured a splash into the pan, lit the gas with a match from the ceramic policeman at the back of the sink, and stirred the red liquid. It began to thin as the heat moved through it, small orange bubbles breaking the surface. She recognized that feeling of thinning with heat. She didn't understand the physics but could catalogue each transition. The initial feeling: cold and thick, stupid and lonely. And then the way her bones vibrated as a boy took her wrists and held them above her head, in the straw, on the concrete behind the garages, on the cobbles by the side of the post office, out of the glare of the lamplight, but lit by the moon. She liked the moon. Liked the way it hit her skin yellow and soft, like wax. That's how she felt with a boy, with her wrists above her head in the moonlight. She felt like a lit candle, alight yet cool at the same time, anticipating the run of wax, the sudden change from cold to hot, the way it was outside her control.

"'Oooooup, 'ooooup!'"

She dropped the spoon on the floor with a clatter, scattering red drops across the lino, and turned in time to see Seamus's blond head dart back under the kitchen table, behind the drop of the tablecloth. Smiling, she picked up the spoon and added another serving into the pan, brought it to a simmer and poured it into two bowls—one for her, Pyrex with black daisies, and one on which Basil the Brush danced foxily around the rim for her little brother. She slid Seamus's bowl across the lino towards his perpetually scabby knees.

"'Red!" He banged the flat of his hand on the lino. "'Red, 'red, 'red, 'red!"

She pulled her slice of bread in two, put half on a saucer and placed it on the floor by her feet. His hand slid out from the shadow of the cloth and dragged the plate back below the table. She listened to him slurping his soup and chewing on the bread. At times, he disgusted her, but now, with the clock ticking the rest of the morning away and the sound of his contented chewing and swallowing from under the table, she felt strangely sisterly.

* * * * *

At teatime, Mrs. O'Flannery was back at the cooker, this time manoeuvring three eggs around a frying pan. At the table, Lilly listened to her brothers kick each other beneath the vinyl cloth. Michael won and banged his fists in victory on the table. Seamus howled.

She was bored. She had been looking forward to the school holidays and now she had wasted the entire first day. Michael had played football since breakfast and was now a happy mess of muddy knees and grass stains. Even Seamus seemed content, traces of his breakfast sausage still evident on the tablecloth. All she had done was sweat in the sun for two hours cleaning out her father's rabbit hutches. Her nose was burnt and her eyelids felt too tight. Plus she had nettle rash on her legs from where she had pushed the wire rabbit run into the sun down by the car port.

She scooted her chair closer to the kitchen table. Its legs screeched on the linoleum, catching on a tear and pulling it wider. She tugged down the hem of her green skirt to stop her skin sticking to the plastic seat.

"What's the difference between tea and dinner, Mum?" she said.

Michael picked up his mug of orange squash and stuck his little finger out. "Tea's in a cup what you drink, and dinner's on a fancy plate!"

"Shut your gob, Arsewipe!" Lilly said. "I'm asking Mum."

Her mother spun round, spatula dripping lard onto the kitchen floor. "Less of the Arsewipe, young lady! And why are you wearing that new skirt?"

Lilly bit her lip. "It's not new. It's secondhand."

"It's new to you, alright? There's kids in Africa who would be proud to have a skirt like that." Her mother picked up a dishcloth from the sink tidy and blotted the fat from the kitchen floor.

Lilly pictured a stick girl with an empty coffee tin gathering water from a well. She wore the green Tonic skirt, and bright beads rattled against her silver neck plates as she wound up the bucket and splashed water into the tin. She had to hurry because her mother was at home cooking fish fingers and rice for tea. Where was Daddy? With the other men, of course. He was sitting outside the chief's tent drinking lager, talking about getting laid and how black ladies' bums stick out a lot.

Her mother rapped the spatula on the table. "Think on, then. And while you're thinking, set the table."

Lilly pulled three bamboo placemats from the drawer and unrolled them. One for her, the one with the black Chinese horses and red letters. One for each of the boys: Michael's— three cowled monks obliterated by congealed tomato sauce, and Seamus's—a bird of paradise. He had unpicked the cotton binding, and the bird's claws were lost in sausage and crumbling bamboo. Seamus, who couldn't say his own name properly, had a knack for taking things apart.

She laid knives and forks on the table and set the tomato ketchup and salt and pepper shakers in the middle.

"Mum, can Nanny crochet?

Her mother shook her head and spooned hot oil on the eggs, their edges turning brown and lacy against the pan. "Lilly, it's as much as your Nan can do to keep her arse clean, let alone do bloody crochet. Who puts these ideas in your head, child?"

"Don't matter," she replied, and traced the outline of the red letters by the side of the galloping horse with the point of her knife.

"Aaaarse," Seamus said, pouring ketchup across the bird's beak and smothering its feathers in salt.

* * * * *

She stroked the hem of her fluffy tank top. Nigel would see her soon. Maybe seven steps more, and she'd be out from beneath the path's canopy of pattering oaks and standing in the sun. They'd all see her. She bit her lips and rubbed her fingers hard across her cheeks, bringing bright spots of colour to her face. The shadow from the trees ended, and she broke out into the long glare of the early evening sun.

He was on his break from the late shift and sat with a group of men on the dry stone wall that skirted the barn on the edge of Trewin's Farm. Even from here, she could see that his Dad's overalls were too big for him. He'd rolled up the legs, but even so, just the toes of his boots poked out the bottom. He was smoking a roll-up, trying to keep it both alight and hanging from the corner of his mouth as he talked. From behind the barn, one of the ink factory's thin chimneys rose high into the sky. Blue and orange smoke stained the clouds that nudged too close to the stack. The roof around the chimney was mended with corrugated iron. It looked like her father's old work trousers, patched through with washed-out colours.

"Hello, Nigel," she mumbled, suddenly shy.

He looked up and took the cigarette from his mouth. He whispered something to the man sitting next to him. The man smiled, his dark skin creasing like an old worn shoe. His hair was long and curly. He looked like a diddicoy, a gypsy. Gypsies stole cars. They pinched lead off church roofs. Her father had told her so.

"Hello, Lilly. What you doing here?"

"I thought I'd come and meet you. Thought maybe we could get some fish and chips?"

"Are you hungry for something hot inside you then, Lilly?" Nigel asked, and the gypsy man threw back his head and laughed. She watched the gold hoop in his ear and the way his curls were all separate like Seamus's when she rinsed his hair in the bathroom on Sunday nights.

"We only had fried egg and beans for our . . . dinner."

Nigel smiled. "And how did little Seamus cope with his dinner then?"

"What do you mean?"

"Well, did he eat it or wear it?" He sniggered.

The gypsy man stood up, rubbed his hands on the front of his overalls, skimming his groin a little too slowly. She sensed the trouble her mother always talked about. She bit her top lip, hid it in her mouth.

"Is this your girlfriend, Nigel?" he asked, not taking his eyes off her.

"Nah, not really. It's just Lilly." Nigel took a sandwich from his lunchbox and crammed half of it into his mouth.

"Pleased to meet you, young lady. You know, you have beautiful eyes." He sounded Irish, like her father. She blushed and fixed her gaze on an imaginary thread on the hem of her skirt.

"You look like an intelligent young lady, Lilly," he said. "Would you say you were intelligent?" The gypsy man cocked his head to one side, his gaze still not wavering. She stopped worrying at the thread that wasn't there, and looked him straight in the eyes. Her father always told her to stare dangerous dogs down.

"I got an 'A' in English."

The man whispered to one of his workmates and laughed. "So, Lilly, do you know the difference between conversation and intercourse?"

"No. We only did stories."

"So then, why don't you lie down here in the grass for a minute, and I'll give you a free lesson." All the men, including

Nigel, burst out laughing, and Lilly, although she didn't know why, felt ashamed and angry. She wished she had a knife, like her father carried when he went fishing down the canal. She'd like to gut that man, stick the knife in his groin. Jag it up to his throat.

Instead, she turned to Nigel. "Do you fancy coming for some chips then?"

"Am I buying?" he said, snapping shut the top of the metal lunchbox.

"I've got no money 'til Friday. I don't get my pocket money 'til then."

"Let's go have a sit in the barn first," he said. "I've not seen you for ages." He put the sandwich box in his overall pocket. "You coming?"

She hitched up her skirt and climbed over the dry-stone wall, grazing her leg on the sharp rocks along the top. The long grass stung her skin. Above her, swallows swooped through the early evening, catching midges and flies, and crying across the telephone wires.

* * * * *

She listened to the birds gossiping high above her in the barn eaves. Nigel pulled up his trousers and tucked in his T-shirt. He stepped into his overalls, then pulled out the sandwich box from his pocket. He took out a sausage roll and bit into it, flakes of pastry dropping to the straw like snow. Lilly's jumper and skirt lay crumpled in the corner. Her knickers were still looped around her ankles. She reached for her abandoned clothes.

"Can we go for chips now, Nigel?"

He stood up and, leaning on the half-door of the barn, turned up the bottoms of his trousers until his boots showed. His head was a halo against the bright sunlight that flooded the meadow outside. He looked like the saint on the stained glass window in the church, all straight lines and blue and gold. She thought she'd marry him when she was old enough. When he asked her.

"What did you think of my mate, Lilly?" he said.

She tugged up her knickers and sat, resting her back against a stall door long left open. "He's alright. Is he a 'diddicoy'?"

He laughed. "He knows his way around." The boy moved out of the sunlight. "He likes you, Lilly," he said with a strange, grown-up smile on his face. "Reckons he could put a word in for me with the boss. Maybe get me a full-time job."

"Yeah?" Lilly pulled the skirt on, adjusting the seams and pulling up the zipper. She picked up the tank top.

"Yeah. Just think, on proper wages, I could take you out somewhere nice. Out to dinner, maybe."

"Dinner? Like at the Sorrento in town?"

"Yeah, why not. We could get a taxi. Do it proper."

The light through the stable door dimmed, and instinctively, she held the jumper up to cover her breasts. She could make out the outline of the gypsy man. The sunlight spun off his curls and jumped a little on the gold hoop in his ear.

"He likes you, Lilly. Don't ya, Carter? D'you like him? He's a chargehand. Like your dad was. He knows everything there is to know about Cobalt Blue."

The man in the sunlight stepped forward and unbuttoned his overalls. Underneath, he wore a string vest. It was brand-new white against his skin.

Nigel left his sandwich box on the floor and walked out into the meadow. She bit her top lip and felt the heat rise through her shins and round to the skin at the back of her knees.

"Nigel?" she called out.

He turned back. "Yeah?"

"La Sorrento, right? Proper dinner?"

"Yeah, Lilly. Proper dinner. Fancy serviettes and everything."

I'm in charge of the 4B Nature Table and every Monday, I have to throw away any dead things and tidy it up. And clean out Edward Heath's cage. He's our hamster. After milk, we go out in the playground and find new nature things. It can't be stuff that's made in shops or anything—like empty Fanta cans or cigarette ends. It has to be something natural—like a conker or a bird egg. Sometimes, Mrs. Tensing asks us to bring in things from home.

Last week, Allan Prince gave me a paper bag and said it was for the nature table. I looked inside, and there was a big pooh in the bottom.

He said he made it himself.

Authentic

❀

Stacey Wright felt she had spent her whole ten years on earth trying to catch up. Especially when it came to fitting into her older sister's hand-me-downs. Of course, she had been fighting a losing battle, what with Janine being six years older, but she'd always dreamed of one day getting to the stage where her sister's castoffs actually fitted her. She remembered the disgrace of having to roll her school skirts over at the waistband, so they didn't drag around her ankles. But her recent growth spurt had proven miraculous. While her hand-me-down school uniform wasn't exactly attractive, at least it now fitted. And sometimes, Janine actually managed to hand over something worth wearing.

She sat in the Stanley Close Spy Club camp wearing just such a castoff. The faded Levis had two lines of orange stitching across the fly placket, five rivets on each of the back pockets, and a red cotton tag just where it should be. They were authentic. For once, in a lifetime of hand-me-downs, Stacey felt good. The Spy Club was an institution for the girls of Stanley Close. Each year at the beginning of the school summer holidays, the girls would gather in the field that ran between the houses of Stanley Close and the council dump and begin work on a hideaway that would last them the entire summer. They would cut branches and weave them into walls. Each girl would scavenge items from home. This year their trove included a green army blanket, a battenberg-checked bath towel, three old china cups and saucers, a vinyl car seat, and a Barbola mirror that had lost the majority of its plaster flowers.

Stacey leant back against the trunk of the huge oak tree that formed the central support of the camp. She stuck her legs straight out in front of her and admired her new jeans. Outside, she could hear Dorothy cutting more branches further along the edge of the field. Here, inside the tree camp, the air was soft and smelt of sap. The dirt floor was still loose and full of insects. By the end of the summer, it would be worn smooth with the slide of their sandals.

A bundle of willow switches landed at her feet, closely followed by Tot who scrambled under the army blanket that served as the camp's portcullis. The younger girl stared at her friend's Levis. "Stacey," she said, "your trousers are bloody lovely. You look like someone off the telly." Tot fingered the triangular insert stitched into the seam of the jeans from knee to hem. "Did *you* make them into flares?"

"No, my sister did it. You see that velvet?"

"Yeah"

"She cut that from Mick Jagger's jacket."

Tot's eyes opened wide. "Did he let her?"

Stacey thought for a moment. "He begged her to. Said he wanted her to have a memento of their night of love."

Tot frowned. "Did they . . . do it then?"

"What?"

"Your Janine and Mick Jagger. Did they, like, did he put his thingy in her?"

"Course not," she said, drawing her knees up to her chest. "It was very romantic. He said their love was like . . . like smoke, but that she was still beautiful and if she liked, she could have his jacket and put it in her jeans, so . . . so she wouldn't forget him." She rubbed the velvet with her thumb. "But you mustn't tell anyone. It's a secret. Because of Bianca."

Tot nodded solemnly and began to weave the whippy willow branches in and out of the bushes and the thin tree trunks that formed the uprights of their camp. The blanket covering the low entrance jerked open again.

"Bianca who?" Dorothy knelt in the entranceway, a bundle of birch twigs in her hand. She had on a spotless blue cheesecloth smock. It was the colour of swimming pools. Over the top, she wore an unbuttoned crocheted waistcoat that looked like a spider's web through a rainbow.

Stacey felt her face and throat burn, not with embarrassment at the possibility of being found out in a lie, but with the emotion she always had when Dorothy arrived in the group. It was the burn of jealousy. She didn't know if it was because Dorothy was beautiful and had long hair that looked like dark water coursing through a lock gate or because her clothes were always so new. Or that she always managed to have done everything before Stacey had either permission or the inclination. Those four years that separated them might have been forty. But still, this envy was tinged with admiration, or perhaps the fine threads of puppy love.

"Bianca who?" Dorothy repeated.

"Mick Jagger's Bianca," Tot said.

"Shut up!" said Stacey. She turned to Dorothy. "Just a girl I know. She doesn't go to your school. I like your waistcoat."

"You can wear it if you want." Dorothy shrugged it off and dropped it on her lap. "This is an Indian broom," she said, holding out the bundle of twigs." We can sweep out all the bugs, and then cover our tracks like squaws."

"Squaw means like a lady's ... front bottom," Tot said.

Stacey stood up and slipped her arms into the waistcoat and said to Dorothy, "She means vagina."

"What means vagina?" asked Dorothy.

"Squaw does," Tot replied, still weaving the birch branches in and out of the tree trunks. The two older girls looked at each other. Stacey shrugged. "It does," Tot said. "Nigel Deepens heard his dad say so."

Dorothy shook her head. "We'll be Indians then. Just plain old Indians."

"We should let Keesal join our club," Tot said.

Dorothy slapped Tot on the head with the bundle of twigs. "NO BOYS!" she said. "And anyway, you're not even in the club."

"And why would you want Keesal to join the club, even if he could?" asked Stacey.

Tot brushed bark out of her kinky hair and scowled at her sister. "Because he's an Indian, and he would know how to do things right. Indian-style."

Dorothy hooted with laughter. "Oh you big spaz! Keesal's from India. That's not the same as being an Indian brave or anything. They come from America. I don't believe you sometimes!" She gathered up the birch twigs and began to sweep the loose dirt floor, while Tot ignored her sister and pulled the bark of the beech branches with her fingernails.

Since Dorothy was the oldest, she had first go with all the new things they made or brought in from home. Stacey watched as she swept the floor free of ants and wilting leaves, and Tot darted in and out of the trunks with her willow switches like a bobbin through a blanket. The light from the August afternoon had become more and more dappled until both girls looked like saplings, and then like girls, and then like waving trees again. She stretched her legs out in front of her and smoothed the long waistcoat out over her thighs.

Dorothy hung the twig broom from a broken branch on the oak tree and pulled out a tin from behind its main trunk. On its lid was a picture of a Scotsman playing the bagpipes. Stacey had brought the tin from home. They'd got it one Christmas and it had been full of shortcake biscuits wrapped in little frilly papers, but now it homed the relics of the Stanley Close Spy Club. Dorothy banged on the lid with a flint to get the meeting to order. "This is the first meeting of the third summer of the Stanley Close Spy Club and I, being Chairman, call this meeting to order."

Stacey and Tot sat up straight.

"This is the holy tin of the Stanley Close Spy Club and as Chairman, it is my tin. I will now pass the tin around to the members for the ritual of *Baise Moi*."

"What ritual of Bays thing?" Tot asked.

Dorothy placed the tin on the ground. "Chris told me about it. He's sixteen and went to Dieppe on an exchange." she said. "It's like swearing an oath or doing a 'cross your heart and hope to die.'"

"Who's Chris?" asked Stacey.

"That's her swanky boyfriend!" Tot said.

"What do you know about anything, anyway!" said Dorothy. She turned to face Stacey. "Inside this holy tin are all our relics and they're . . . they're important, right?"

Stacey nodded.

"What are relics?" Tot asked.

"So, we pass the tin around and kiss the lid and promise to guard the relics with our lives and the lives of our Mums and any animals we have. That's the ritual of *Baise Moi.*"

"And the life of your boyfriend. If you've got one," Tot added.

"Oh, shut up!" Dorothy said.

"Alright, alright! Keep your hair on! So the Bays thing is just promising?" Tot asked.

"Of course not, Spaz! If it was just promising, we'd just do 'Cross Your Heart' or something. *Baise Moi* means that if you say it and kiss the lid and then you fuck up—"

Tot gasped. "That's the 'Big Girl's Word'! You can't say that!"

"And that's why this is a big girls' club and you shouldn't even be here. Do you want to know or what?"

Tod nodded.

"As I was saying, if you fuck up and don't protect the relics, you have to promise to let anyone . . . " Dorothy thought for a moment. "Kiss you or ravage you, or . . . or like, do bad stuff even if you're kicking and saying no and things. It's that bad."

"Like rape?" asked Stacey.

"No, not as bad as rape. But like . . . like in the films."

"So why do we have to say that?" Tot asked.

"You don't," said Dorothy. "You're not a member. You're just here because Mum's gone to the shops and won't let you stay in the house on your own."

"My mum let me stay in the house when I was little," Stacey said.

"Can I see the relics, Stacey?" asked Tot.

Dorothy ignored her. "My mum says that's irresponsible. I'm all right because I'm fourteen, but Tot's only eight, and she's got epilepsy."

"I get fits," said Tot. "They're icky, and I go like this." She jerked her arms and legs around and made her eyes cross over.

"Don't do that!" said Dorothy. "You'll get one, and then I'll have to take you home." Tot stopped jerking. "We have to do *Baise Moi* to protect the relics. Like I said. It's the same as 'cross my heart and hope to die' and stuff. Here." She shoved the biscuit tin towards Stacey. "Kiss it."

"Bays m-war" she said, kissing the Scotsman on the tin lid.

"D'ya like her jeans, Dorothy?" Tot asked.

"They're all right."

Stacey cradled the Scotsman in her lap.

"Mum doesn't let us wear jeans," Tot told Stacey.

Dorothy glared at her younger sister. "Yes, she does. Just not blue ones."

"Or black ones," Tot said.

"No."

"Or green ones, or red ones, or pink ones—"

"SHUT YOUR GOB!" Dorothy said and threw a handful of dirt at Tot.

Tot coughed and wiped the dust from her eyes. "When I grow up, I'm going to have jeans like Stacey's. I'm not going to wear skirts, or bloody baggy dresses or STUPID SPIDER WEB THINGS."

"It's not stupid. Nanny crocheted it." Dorothy put her arm around Stacey's shoulder. "Don't look at her! She's not even in the club. And don't say bloody or I'll tell mum on you"

"Well, you just said 'fuck.' Anyway, I HATE YOU!" Tot picked up a rock and threw it at Dorothy. It hit her on her cheek, an inch below her eye. Dorothy clamped her hand over her face. Tot looked shocked, and Stacey didn't know whether to smack Tot in the mouth for attacking a club member or burst into tears.

Dorothy lowered her hand, and a thin line of blood crept down her face towards the corner of her mouth. "You wait, you bloody little bugger! You wait till mum gets home!" Dorothy disappeared out the entrance, the blanket flapping behind her.

Stacey looked across at Tot, who was trying very hard not to cry. "Do you want to see the relics, Tot?" she asked. Tot nodded and crawled over to sit next to Stacey. Stacey opened the lid.

* * * * *

For the next ten minutes, Stacey and Tot pretended to be busy. They were aware that a storm could hit their camp at any moment—either in the form of a returning Dorothy or the arrival of Tot's mum. Stacey scraped a hole behind the tree in which to conceal the relic tin, and Tot collected a stash of rocks and stones in case of invaders. They were interrupted by Dorothy jerking back the door blanket.

She scuttled into the camp on her knees. Once in, she sat back on her heels and shook her head at the two girls. She wore a pink plaster over her cheek and was carrying a Sainsbury's carrier bag. "You didn't even hear me!" she said. "I could have been anyone. I could have been a nutter from the hospital or . . . or Seamus!"

"Sorry," Stacey replied. "I was burying the tin."

"And I'm not a member," said Tot. "So I don't even have to be a look-out or anything."

"Shut up! I'm still not talking to you!" Dorothy turned to Stacey and pulled a shiny brass trumpet from her bag.

"You've got Dad's trumpet!" Tot cried. "I'm telling. You can't!"

"Why not? He's not using it."

"He told me to look after it for him."

"Well, you've done a crappy job, haven't you?" Dorothy pulled a leather pouch from her pocket and took out the brass mouthpiece. "Now, if we see any invaders coming, we can blow the trumpet, and if you're outside the camp, foraging or spying, you'll know to come back here and . . . repel people."

Stacey looked at the golden instrument in Dorothy's lap. Before Mr. Thompson left for America, she had listened to him practicing. Every Sunday at 10:30 AM, clutching his black leather trumpet case, he'd walk across the Green on his way to The Eagle in the village to play with The Blue Notes. In the summer, he wore his stripy blazer and straw hat. Her father didn't really like him. He said Mr. Thompson was a "rich bastard." And worse. "Any man who wears a straw hat," he said, "is a poof in my book."

"Why didn't he take it with him?" she asked.

"Because this is only an old beginner's trumpet," said Dorothy, "and Uncle Trevor bought him a new one when he got to New Orleans."

"Like Dizzy Gillespie's," Tot mumbled.

"Are you going to keep the trumpet in the tree?" Stacey asked.

"Of course not! It might only be a beginner's one, but it's worth lots of money. I'll bring it with me." Dorothy screwed the brass mouthpiece in place. "I'm the only one allowed to blow it."

Stacey looked down and saw Tot stroking the nap of the velvet triangular insert in her jeans with a twig. Aware she was being watched, she dropped the stick. She said "Sorry," and Stacey noticed she was crying.

"S'all right," she replied. "You can carry on if you want."

Tot retrieved her stick and brushed the nap one way shiny and then the other way matt. "It's like Barney's fur," Tot said. "I'm going to have jeans like this. One day," she said, "I'm going to have velvet in my jeans, like Stacey, and live in Norleans."

Stacey smiled. Dorothy's trumpet didn't seem quite so special any more. "I've put something in the Spy Log," Stacey said.

Dorothy looked up. "What?"

She dragged the shortbread tin out of its hiding place, opened it, and handed a spiral-bound notebook to Dorothy. She took it and flipped through to the latest entry and read aloud what Stacey had written. "Monday 18th August 1972. Forty-three minutes past seven. Janine let . . . what's that say, Stacey?" Dorothy pointed to a word.

She leant over the notebook. "Barry Mountain."

"Oh, right." Dorothy continued to read aloud. "Janine let Barry Mountain put his hand up her jumper. Janine and Barry on sofa in front room. Janine wearing red jumper. Barry wearing jeans, black Ben Sherman and boxer boots. Barry had hand up her jumper for two minutes. Janine went into kitchen and came back with two cups. Mum and dad back in Close at forty-nine minutes past seven. Barry out dining room window at fifty minutes past seven." Dorothy closed the book. "You didn't say where you were spying from."

"I was in the front garden under the window." Stacey said. "By the laburnum tree."

"Yeah, but you didn't write that. And you didn't say how you did it." Dorothy shook her head.

"What do you mean?"

"Like if it was through a window or what."

Stacey thought for a moment. "I hooked the net curtains around the back of the fruit bowl, and then went outside."

"You should have put that in the book." Dorothy said. "It's what the book's for."

Tot stopped stroking Stacey's jeans. "Did she have a bra on?" she asked. Stacey shook her head. "What was in the mugs?"

Dorothy put the book in the tin, and slid it back in the hole. She picked up the trumpet and blew a quivering, scratchy note. The branches above them shook, and Stacey felt as if the sky was brimming with birds flying and calling.

"It might have been whiskey," she told Tot.

"That's nothing." Dorothy stroked the trumpet in her lap. "I saw something that you don't know about."

"What?" they both asked.

"Something about someone who's in this club. And Tot Thompson, you can't say nothing any more, because you're not a member, and if you do, I'm going to tell Mum that you've been talking to Dad on the phone."

Tot considered what her sister had said for a moment. "I'm not going home though. Mum said you had to look after me."

"And I will, but you're not to talk from now on, all right?" Tot nodded and picked up her stick again. "You shouldn't even listen really."

Dorothy turned to Stacey. "Do you want to know?" Stacey nodded. "It's better than your spying, because this is about a member and someone else who we know. Someone's whose name begins with N. Someone who Tot fancies."

Tot blushed.

"Nigel?" asked Stacey.

"Yeah, Nigel and . . . someone in Stanley Close whose name begins with an L."

"Lilly?" Tot said, looking up from the dirt.

"I said you had to keep your mouth shut!"

Tot bit her lip and dug at the dirt floor with a stick. "I want to see the relics," she said. "Stacey, can I see the relics again?"

"Shut up about the relics," said Dorothy. "Did you show her the relics?" she asked Stacey. "She's not even a member!"

"It was Lilly though, right?" Stacey asked.

"Yeah." Dorothy studied the toe of her shoe.

"What then?" asked Stacey.

"You wanna know?"

"Yes!"

"I saw Lilly and Nigel doing it in the barn on Springhouse Way." Tot snapped her stick. "I was spying. And that's not all."

"What? Tell me! What happened?" Stacey asked.

"Then she did it with a man. She did it with a gypsy man from the factory."

"What, like a grown up?"

"Yeah. He was old. It was disgusting!"

"What did she do?" asked Stacey.

"She was lying there, like underneath, and he was on top making noises."

"What kind of noises?"

"Like . . . like he was having a big pooh or something."

"Why was he having a pooh?" asked Tot.

"He wasn't, Spaz!" Dorothy threw a twig at Tot.

"What happened then?" asked Stacey.

"Then he got off."

The three girls were silent. Dorothy, smiling broadly at the magnitude of what she had reported, grabbed the spiral-bound book from the half-buried biscuit tin, pulled a pencil from her skirt pocket, and began to write frantically.

Tot searched around in the bushes for another twig. "Lilly knows things," she said.

Stacey wished that her sister had done something more with Barry Mountain than just let him touch her up. Every time I get something good, she thought, Dorothy comes up with something better. She looked down at her jeans and noticed the hem was coming undone. The velvet was fraying at the back. Tot pulled the bark off another twig and buried it in the dust around the oak roots. It was quiet. There was just the sound of Dorothy's pencil on the paper and a faint calling of seagulls from the dump.

Stacey carefully pulled at a thread that hung from the bottom of her jeans. It unravelled, and a small pile of burgundy fibres fell to the ground next to her foot. "That's what my cousin does when he's babysitting me," Stacey said. "He puts the sofa against the front room door so his little sisters can't come in, and then we do it. In front of the gas fire." She pulled at another thread. "Like Lilly and the gypsy man. We do that ALL the time." Dorothy and Tot both looked at her. "We do!" she repeated. "But it's all right because I don't have periods, so I won't get a bun in the oven. My cousin told me."

The silence fell heavy in the small space beneath the oak, all woven through with stripped beech branches. Tot got up first and slipped through a hole in the branch wall. Stacey could hear her crying as she made her way along the line of trees that skirted the rubbish dump.

Dorothy stood and picked up the trumpet. "This club's stupid!" she said. "I'm not hanging around with stupid little liars like you anymore." She reached up and undid the clothes pegs that held the doorway blanket in place. "And I'm taking this home as well!" She threw the blanket over her shoulder, then disappeared out the opening into the field.

Stacey watched her moving through the uncut meadow. Her blue dress was almost shrouded by the dull green army blanket. Then she was lost in the long yellowing grasses that grew along the wire-link fence at the edge of the aerodrome. She nudged the shortbread tin with the toe of her plimsoll. Way off in the distance, she could hear a dustcart engine, could hear its gears and the whine of the engine as it struggled up the incline to the top of the hill. The air outside was filled with the sound of seagulls, all shrieking in hungry anticipation as the dustcart emptied its load of litter and leftovers into the tip.

My sister's nearly a woman. She's got a boyfriend and a whole dot-to-dot of spots. She gets new ones every week.

She and I don't share knickers anymore. She's got new ones with skinny side straps, and they're covered in little roses. I don't mind, because I've got twice as many pants all to myself now.

She's got three bras that stand up all on their own. I can get a knee in each cup. Mum could use them as kneeling pads when she weeds the garden.

When Dorothy has a bath, I look through the keyhole. She's got really big busties now, a huge bum and her tummy sticks out like she's swallowed a whole Fray Bentos kidney pudding. Mum said it was probably puppy fat.

All this growing up is making my sister sick. I hear her puking up every morning round the back of the potting shed.

My best pants have got trains on them.

Herbaceous Perennials

❁

Dorothy lay reading in the meadow next to the aerodrome. Above, the Goodyear airship hung in the sky like a bloated silver sow grazing on clouds. Occasionally, its motors fired, and it retreated slowly back to the sky above the airfield. Each time, the noise from the engines lifted a chorus of gulls from the rubbish dump that lay between the semi-detached houses of Stanley Close and the aerodrome. Lilly had told her that seagulls know if someone is expecting a baby. She said if a pregnant woman floats on her back in the ocean, the gulls circle like vultures over something dead and scream her name to the waves.

She put down the book to watch the gulls wheeling and swooping. Behind them, two dustcarts emptied their loads into the deep landfill pits. An endless stream of black plastic bags tumbled out, some ripping on the carts' jaws and spilling a week's worth of rubbish across the dark soil. The gulls bitched and screamed, each determined to seize whatever edibles might lurk among the nappies, packaging and leftovers.

She heard the unmistakeable sound of Tot's laughter piercing through the scavenging bird calls and raised herself up on her elbows. Tot and Keesal Patel were walking along the pathway that ran along the edge of the field. They both had fishing nets over their shoulders and Tot, walking backwards, was pointing out different landmarks to the skinny little Indian boy. She watched Tot point out the tyre swing over the gully by the copse, she showed him the sloe tree, the Burning Bush by the entrance to the dump. And then Tot pointed out the Spy Camp.

Dorothy didn't care. Her legs ached and her breakfast churned in her stomach. Some days, she didn't care about anything. She picked up the book and continued to read.

It wasn't the usual type of thing she read. She was a fan of *Seventeen* and *Jackie*, and took part in every survey. She poured over each article for tips on knockout makeup and how to impress boys. They were the mother lode she mined for answers, but both magazines had came up empty on her current dilemma. They offered counsel only up to the point of snaring the boy. They didn't tell you "Five Crazy Ways to Tell Him You're Pregnant," or "Top Ten Ways to Make Him Marry You." She could have asked Anna Raeburn at Capital Radio for advice, but knew it would involve coming clean with her mother, or going it alone somehow. And her mother, an avid Raeburn fan, might recognise her voice. Then, if her mum found out, her Dad would know, and her grandmother and pretty soon, the cat would be out of the bag and caterwauling all around Stanley Close.

The book was entitled "Herbs: A Complete Guide to their Cultivation and Use." The cultivation aspect of the book was by-the-by—there was no room for herbs in the Thompson's small, square back garden. There was already the rampant mint patch that threatened her father's dahlias. And even the mint had no real use, apart for flavouring the lamb every fourth Sunday. She raised the book and blocked out the airship.

* * * * *

Dorothy lay wedged in the empty tub. Her bare shoulders were jammed against one side of the bath and her lower back and buttocks against the other. Her legs stuck straight up the tiled wall, calves resting against the clammy white tiles. She was wrapped in a dark green towel, but she was cold.

Lilly sat on the laundry basket and pulled a can of Orange Fanta from her bag. Dorothy watched her set it down in the wire bath tidy next to a moth-eaten natural sea sponge. The whole situation felt entirely unfair to her. It should be Lilly stuck on the Bishop's Croft housing estate with a late period, not her. Lilly's big, coarse mother and unemployed father wouldn't have given a damn if she came home pregnant with twins. But instead it was Dorothy who was propped up and shivering in the bathtub, looking through tears at a re-run of her mother's wasted life: pregnant and proud owner of a Bishop's Croft rent book.

"You said it had to be Coca Cola," Dorothy said. "And in a bottle."

"And I also said you had to do it straight afterwards." Lilly picked up the can and shook it. "When did you do it with him?"

Dorothy was silent.

"Well look, it's worth a try," Lilly said. "It's got to be better than all those bloody herbs you keep chewing. You're going to have to open your legs though."

"Couldn't we use one of your Mum's douche things?" asked Dorothy.

"Nah, it's in their bedroom, and I'm not allowed in there. You'll just have to try and pour it.

"Should I shake it again?"

"I don't know. I've never done this before. I just heard about it."

"Well, don't look!" Dorothy said.

Lilly turned to face the wall, and Dorothy took the can and shook it hard. She snapped back the ring-pull, and upended it between her legs.

She felt the bubbles explode against the skin of her thighs and a cool rush of liquid fizzed across her stomach. It felt like Space Dust. It felt a lot better than Chris had, with his thick, sticky fingers, him grunting and pushing against her. She had thought it was romantic, what with the moon and the owl skimming across the water. She should have known it was all going to turn to shit when they'd heard that boy pissing behind them.

"Can I turn round yet?" Lilly asked. "Have you done it?"

"Yeah, but I don't think it worked."

Lilly fussed at her hair in the mirror above the basin, but Dorothy could tell she was watching her in the mirror's reflection. "Throw me another towel," Dorothy said and Lilly pulled one from the towel rail. Still wedged into the tub, she draped the towel over herself.

"Can I touch it?" Lilly asked.

"Touch what?"

"The baby."

Lilly's words transformed the "pregnancy" into a baby. The hard lump, the problem, the thing that must be got rid of became a crying, kicking, cooing baby. Dorothy nodded and drew back the towel, exposing her swollen stomach. Lilly's hand was hot and stuck to her skin.

"I thought you'd be bigger," Lilly said. "My Dad's rabbits get huge when they're expecting. How far along are you? How many months?"

"Six."

Lilly rinsed her hand under the tap. "I think it's too late, Dorothy. You ought to tell your mum. She probably knows already."

Dorothy shook her head. "She doesn't. She doesn't notice anything since Dad left."

"She hasn't said anything?"

"No. It's been easy really. I've been wearing smocks and loose things. Keeping my coat on and that."

"What about Tot?"

"She's too little to understand. She thinks I'm just getting fat." Dorothy lowered her legs into the tub.

Lilly stopped her. "You need to stay like that for a while," she said.

"How long?"

"I don't know. Ten minutes maybe." Lilly dried her hands. "You fancy going up the village later on. There's a group playing at the youth club."

"S'pose." Dorothy wrapped the towel tightly around her. She thought about Chris and how he wouldn't marry her. He'd called her a dirty scrubber and taken his jacket back. She looked at Lilly. "You won't tell anyone, will you?"

"Cross my heart."

"And thanks."

"What for?"

"For the orange."

"S'all right," Lilly said, closing the bathroom door behind her.

* * * * *

The airship was moving gently above her, nudging its shiny nose out from behind the red covers of her book, and then retreating and showing her its silver tail fins. She spread out her arms, cruciform in the long grass, her blue cheesecloth smock bunching up over the long meadow grass. She held the red book in one hand and in the other, a spray of yellow flowers, each head as round as a button, as bright as egg yolks. A handful of Yellow Tansy. *Tanacetum Vulgare*, an Herbaceous Perennial.

She had begun to memorise the words from the book of herbs, reciting them like prayers. She whispered them in the darkness of her bedroom before she went to sleep. She began with the safe herbs, the ones destined for salads and Sunday chickens. "Sweet Cicely," she'd say, swaddling herself tight beneath the crocheted bedspread. "*Myrrhis Odorata*, with its delicate leaves, smells of myrrh." She pictured it sweetening the manger. "Tarragon," she'd continue, switching off the light. "*Artemisia Dracunculus*. Latin for little dragon. It was thought to heal the bite of serpents."

The Goodyear airship criss-crossed the meadow once more, and she was cast into shadow. She placed one frond of the tansy between the book's pages and began to slowly chew each of the yellow button flowers. They were tart, but not as sour as the springy green fronds, each one a mouthful of bitterness.

The gulls were beginning to roost and perched incongruously in the beech trees. No groins or pilings for these birds. No ship's rigging or bare rocks to sleep on. She swallowed and began the tale of Tansy. A bedtime story for gulls. A tale to rival Grimms. "*Tanacetum Vulgare*, fresh or dried in small quantities to help digestion, and to help in the treatment of roundworms. Large quantities harmful." She rubbed her mouth with the back of her hand. "None should be taken in pregnancy."

All along the copse where the Tansy grew, there were tangles of chickweed and nettles. Everywhere there were nettles. She remembered her grandmother telling her to always grasp them firmly and promising that if she did as she was told, they wouldn't sting. They always did.

* * * * *

Saturday morning. Mum was at Sainsbury's and Tot was out. Probably back at the canal fishing for minnows, thought Dorothy. She slipped the round brown kernel and the tin grater into her dressing gown pocket. Lilly had warned her that the nutmeg on its own would be useless. She had to take it with gin.

In the dining room, she knelt on the carpet in front of the G-Plan cabinet. All of the cupboards in the cabinet were out of bounds for Dorothy, but given the fact that gin was essential, it would have to be another rule she broke. Her dad used to call the middle section "The Cocktail Cabinet." Her mum said that was pretentious, but he kept doing it anyway. Dorothy pulled down the door. On the top shelf, reflected in the mirrored back, was the party set: thick-bottomed tumblers, eight thin-stemmed wine glasses, a small, buttoned leather pouch containing enamelled spirit measures, a jar of maraschino cherries and a sealed packet of cocktail sticks. On the right, on the bottom shelf, were the other glasses—blue half-pints, a handled beer mug and three straight-sided pint glasses. On the left were the spirits: Blue Curacao someone from work had given her Dad, a bottle of sherry from last Christmas, half a bottle of Bells, a soda siphon and a promotional decanter of Dry Gordon's gin.

She pulled out the decanter and lifted off the heavy glass stopper. Carefully, she poured the clear liquid into the beer mug, then topped up the bottle from the soda siphon. The gin fizzed and bubbled for a moment and then settled back down behind the label that showed the head of a red boar snarling over a line of juniper berries.

She closed the cupboard door and climbed the stairs to the bathroom where she had drawn a deep bath. She placed the beer mug and nutmeg grater into the wire tidy and watched the last few drops drip from the tap and ripple the surface. It was ironic, she thought, how this whole thing had begun with water. She stepped into the bath. The near-scalding water caused her skin to flush crimson and tears to well in her eyes. Bracing herself with her feet against the tap end, she took a long swig of the gin. She took the nutmeg from the tidy and began to rasp it against the sharp metal teeth of the grater. A stream of brown dust fell into the palm of her hand. She licked it. It tasted like Christmas.

* * * * *

The grass was damp and the gentle rain of the late afternoon had sent the gulls to roost early. In the aerodrome, the airship had been tethered for the evening, and Dorothy could hear it bouncing against its ropes. She closed her eyes and saw the boar in red relief against the inside of her eyelids.

"Pennyroyal. *Mentha Pulegium Decumbens*, an herbaceous perennial. If strewn, will discourage fleas and ticks. Prefers a moist soil and can be found near ponds and streams. Should not be used where kidney disease is present or in pregnancy."

She stared at the picture. Sprays of pennyroyal crept across the page; beautiful mauve flowers clustered like clover from where the leaves spread on either side of the thick, fibrous stem.

But there was no pennyroyal in the copse with the chickweed and nettles. There was none to be found in the ocean of black bin bags, rusting fridges, the endless O's of car tyres on the dump. The racks of herbs in the village store contained parsley, turmeric, sage, and basil. Even nutmeg. But no pennyroyal.

Dorothy stood up, leaving the book behind in the grass that had already yellowed in the late summer heat. She ran her hands down the front of her smock, as if trying to discover the shape of the thing that would not be dislodged. In the trees around her, the gulls had already roosted and one bird, younger than the others, stretched out its pale brown wings and beat the air as if considering flight. It hopped once on the bough, then tucked its head back below its wing and was still.

Autumn 1972

Paint-by-Numbers are brilliant. I used to get one every Christmas AND every birthday. I've done dolphins and countryside and horses. Last year, I got the Queen.

They don't just give you the shape of the thing, like "here's a dolphin shape," but they give you the shape of the colours ON the thing. A dolphin isn't really gray. It's blue and mauve and brown. It's even got some yellow on it. Once you do a Paint-by-Numbers, you never see things the same again.

I don't get them any more. Last Christmas, I swapped round all the colours and turned Queen Elizabeth into a black lady, like Mrs. Patel. Mum said it was disrespectful, but Mrs. Patel liked it. She said I was "peculiar" and gave me a Kit-Kat.

"Peculiar" is Indian for "good at painting."

Wild Plum and Rainbow Slides

❁

When Barbie did the splits, her plastic feet touched either side of one bamboo square on the Japanese print linoleum. Hidden from view under the kitchen table, Stacey moved Barbie around, measuring the world in terms of her plastic body. Her arms stretched across five bamboo canes, and her waist was the width of a lotus leaf. One foot was the exact length of the hole in her mother's tights. She scuttled backwards as Mrs. O'Flannery from number seven crossed her legs. Stacey stroked Barbie's smooth leg and decided that when she grew up, she wouldn't have holes in her tights.

"So, Pat, when's Noreen and the baby coming out?" She could hear Mrs. O'Flannery stirring her tea.

"Not for a week," her mother replied. Then, in a low voice as if telling a secret, she said, "Apparently, they went a bit far with the stitching."

"What do you mean?"

"Well, she tore so badly—front and back—when the surgeon sewed her up, he stitched over her clitoris."

Mrs. O'Flannery uncrossed her legs and pressed her knees together.

Her mother continued. "They've got to slit her open and redo it."

"Poor woman!"

Stacey sat Barbie in the pink plastic armchair and clipped the *diamanté* tiara in her hair. Pretty. She wished she had a tiara. She wished she were a princess. She heard the snap of a lighter and the sound of Mrs. O'Flannery dragging deep on a cigarette. Stacey picked up a tiny silver shoe.

"I heard the baby was nine pounds and breach. Husband reckoned he'd not seen so much blood since they hit that sheep on the way back from Jaywick."

The shoe refused to fit the foot.

"Stupid sod, he shouldn't have been there. I don't hold with husbands in the delivery room." Stacey heard her mother's cup rattle in its saucer.

"Poor cow," Mrs. O'Flannery said. "She's not had much of a life, has she?" Stacey studied Mrs. O'Flannery's platform shoes. Raffia soles and pale blue straps. Sparkly.

"Have any of us?" Her mother slowly rubbed the back of her calf with the toe of her pink fun fur slipper. "As my old mum used to say, 'First the blood and then the pain!' I used to think she was joking, laying it on. But you know, Vee, after twenty years of periods, two kids and then a year to get over the hysterectomy, I don't think I've had a lovely life either. Have you?"

Stacey considered twenty years of periods. Twenty times twelve. Her mother had said to let her know if there was ever blood in the toilet. She checked, but there never was. She thought about the stitched-up lady and the surgeon slitting her open like a letter. Barbie's tiara fell off and landed in a tangle of dust in the corner by the dog's basket. She heard her mother pouring more tea.

"Men!" said Mrs. O'Flannery. "If they sink seven pints on a Friday night, they think they're man of the year!"

That sounded better. Her dad took her to The Broken Staff last summer. It was full of men talking and laughing too loud.

She had liked the blue layers of cigarette smoke and remembered stroking a whippet, the nubs of his spine hard through the brindle fur.

"And they're right, aren't they? You know, if I come back, I'm coming back as a man. Let someone else have a go at being a woman."

Stacey agreed. She clipped the tiara back on Barbie's head. She'd rather have the beer and the cigarette smoke and the skinny dog with its knobbly back.

* * * * *

Her sister spread sparkles on her cheekbones with a large soft brush and pouted in the mirror. Stacey sat on her bed and watched as Janine slipped into a cheesecloth gypsy top. A line of tin bells stitched along the hem of the wide angel sleeves tinkled.

"Will you stop looking at me!" Janine glared at her through the mirror.

Stacey looked away and turned the page of her magazine. "I'm not."

"You are. Stop it."

"Can't make me."

Janine zipped her jeans and checked her rear end in the mirror. "Haven't you got any worms to dig up or anything?"

Stacey put down the magazine. "Janine?"

Her sister threw the brush down on the dressing table with a clatter. "What!"

"Have you done it . . . all the way with a boy, I mean?" She watched Janine in the glass and thought about her sister making babies and being a woman. She remembered the dog in the pub and her father laughing and the way her aunt pressed her legs together. She wondered what breach meant.

"Well . . . I haven't," Janine said, "but Katie Burgess did it last summer with a French exchange student."

"Did she say what it was like?"

Janine smiled in the mirror. "Kate said his willy was huge, and that it really hurt, and there was so much blood on the sofa, she had to tell her mum the cat killed a rabbit on it."

"Why was there blood on the sofa?"

"Oh my God! Don't you know anything? Because he stuck his big fat cock in her and ripped her insides open. God, you are a spazmo!" Janine picked up the brush again and ran it slowly through her hair. "When I do it," she said, "I'm going to do it properly . . . in a bed-and-breakfast or something."

* * * * *

From a cubicle in the ladies' toilet at the Bishop's Croft recreation field, Stacey could hear the sound of the football match. She tore a square of toilet tissue from the roll and separated the two sheets. She could hear Tot humming quietly in the next cubicle. She carried on with her story. "And then Janine said that they rip your insides out with their thingy and that there's blood everywhere . . . enough to fill a rabbit."

Tot stopped humming. "A whole rabbit's worth?"

"A whole rabbit. And my mum said there's no way she's being a woman again, and she should know, what with me and Janine and the histal-rectomy."

"And it all starts when you get a period?"

Stacey dropped the paper into the toilet bowl between her legs. It floated for a moment, then sank. "It starts with periods, and they're full of blood too, and my sister says they hurt like someone's sticking knives up your front bottom, and you can't go swimming or wear skirts because you smell like old fish, and if you do wear a skirt, everyone will know and the boys will point at you."

She could hear the crowd cheering and the clank of the chains on the swings.

Tot flushed the toilet. "But you get to wear makeup then, yeah? My sister says you get to do loads of stuff when you're older, like fourteen. And starting your periods is older, right? You can wear makeup and go out with boys and things. Maybe get your own flat?"

She could see Tot's shoe. Her sock had pink lace around the ribbing. Pretty. "I don't want my own flat," she said, "and I don't want boys sticking their things in me. I'm not going to do it. I've decided." They were pretty, but she didn't need socks like that.

"You have to." Tot picked at the lace with her fingers. "It's nature and . . . God and everything."

"I'm not going to. From now on, from right now, I'm going to be a boy."

Tot stopped picking. "What's your name, then?"

"Roger."

"Like the Dodger?"

"No. Like our dog."

"You can't call yourself after your dog."

"Why not? I like our dog." She thought about Roger and how he could lick his privates, and how her dad and Mr. O'Flannery said they wished they were Roger.

"Well, what about when your dad takes the dog for a walk, and he calls out, 'Come on, Roger, time for a walk!' You'll think he's talking to you."

That could be a problem, she thought. Then again, her dad never took Roger for a walk.

"And what about when he says, 'Roger, get off the sofa' or 'Roger, you've done a big pooh on the grass!'"

Stacey snorted at the image, and they both dissolved into a giggling fit.

Tot recovered first, her voice breathless and nasal, like she had a cold. "What about David?"

"David?"

"After David Essex. Or David Bowie?"

David was a nice name. Her cousin was called David. He had green eyes and lived in Greenstead. Last summer, they'd gone to visit. Her mum and dad and Auntie Norma and Uncle Joe had all gone to the pub. David locked his little sisters in the kitchen while he and Stacey played Doctors and Nurses in the front room. She had a crush on him ever since. She knew it was a crush, because every time she saw him, her stomach went hot, like she'd eaten too much chicken casserole.

"All right then. David." Stacey pulled up her knickers.

"David?" said Tot.

"What?"

"You know you said you were going to be a boy from this minute?"

"Yeah," Stacey said, reaching for the toilet chain.

"You can't. Not from right now."

"Why not?"

"You've got a skirt on."

She looked down at the skirt bunched up around her waist. "From tomorrow then," she said. "Do you want to see something?" She stood on the toilet seat and peered over the cubicle wall. Tot nodded. She unbuttoned her shirt and pulled up her vest to reveal her chest which was swaddled in a salmon-pink crêpe bandage.

Tot clamped her hands over her mouth in horror. "Have you cut your titties off, Stacey?"

"It's David!" she said. "No. I've just bandaged them up."

"Why?"

She re-buttoned her blouse. "Because boys don't have boobies."

"I don't either," said Tot.

"That's because you're only eight and I'm ten and big boned." Stacey climbed down from the toilet seat and flushed. "It's what man-lesbians do. I saw it on the telly."

Tot called over the noise of the cistern. "You're not a lesbian, are you, David?"

"No, don't be silly. I'm a boy."

* * * * *

It was Saturday afternoon, and Stacey and her father sat on the sofa watching *Match of the Day*. Her mother was sewing at the gateleg table in the bay window. Stacey wore her father's slippers. They were brown tartan and very old. She liked the feel of them on her feet and could feel the rubber of the sole through her thin sock. Stacey linked her arm in her father's. His was muscled and hairy. Even the backs of his hands were hairy. He tipped his beer can and belched. "That was never offside, Ref!" He crushed the can and dropped it on the floor by the side of the sofa. The dog sniffed it, licked the carpet, and went back to sleep. "Jesus! Did you see that, Pat?" Her mother didn't reply. "Bloody referee gave an offside! Christ, Stacey could do a better job than that bastard."

She smiled and pushed her toes deeper into his slippers. Her father scratched his groin and belched again. She reached down between her own legs and scratched contentedly. He laughed at her and ruffled her hair. She liked it when he did that. It made her feel special.

The whine of the sewing machine cut through the noise of the football match on the television. Her father leant forward to turn up the volume. "What are you making, Pat?" he asked, not taking his eyes from the television screen.

"It's a dress for Stacey."

She looked at the pink fabric running beneath the needle of the sewing machine. The material was shiny, but she knew it would scratch.

Her mother continued. "I can't have Stacey parading around at Janine's sixteenth in old clothes. Not with our Norma's girls looking like they just stepped out of Laura Ashley's."

Her mother gunned the sewing machine.

"Pat," her father said, "I can't hear the telly! Can't you make the bloody dress in the kitchen?"

"Bloody dress," Stacey swore under her breath.

* * * * *

She was right. The dress was scratchy. "I don't want to wear the stupid dress!"

Her mother slapped her hard on the leg. "This is ridiculous! Just put it on. I need to hem it."

Stacey threw herself backwards on the bed and stuck out her arms and legs like a starfish. She spread her legs wider, one foot on the wall and one on the bedside cabinet. Like Barbie.

"Get up right now, young lady. I'll count to three, and if you're not wearing this dress, you can kiss goodbye to next month's pocket money!"

A whole month? She needed things. She needed trousers. She needed . . . shaving foam. She sat up. "I can't wear it! You don't understand. I can't wear dresses any more."

Her mother's face looked grim. "I don't care what the fashion is this week. I've made this dress, and you're damn well going to wear it. No more discussion."

She handed it to Stacey who held it in her lap. She hated pink. She wanted Oxford Bags like the Bay City Rollers. She didn't want blood in the toilet. She felt the lump in her throat harden as her mother sat down on the bed.

"Sweetheart, you loved this dress two weeks ago. You chose the fabric and the pattern . . . come on, dry your eyes."

Stacey wiped her eyes on the shiny pink material.

"Not on the dress!" Her mother stood up. "Just put it on for a minute or two. That's all it will take. A couple of minutes, a handful of pins, and you're done."

She looked at the pink dress in her lap. "Just for a minute?"

"Two at the most."

She stood up and raised her arms, and her mother slipped the dress down over her head. She looked at her reflection in the mirror. She watched herself turning into pink and her mother, a mouth full of pins, smiling that sharp smile.

"Look at my little princess. You look so pretty, Stacey. I can't believe it. My little girl almost grown up!"

* * * * *

Stacey sat on the back door step and watched her mother sewing. Her mother hummed the theme tune from the Archers as she stitched the hem of the pink dress. On the table, next to the red felt strawberry pin cushion, was a miniature version for Barbie. A matching pair.

* * * * *

When Tot handed Stacey the grey twill trousers, Age 9-11, in a Sainsbury's bag, Stacey asked her where she had got them. Tot merely said she had borrowed them, and that they just needed a press. Stacey unplugged the steam iron and shook out the trousers. They were a bit big, but they'd do. She stepped into them, and buttoned her school blouse over the pink bandages. The trousers looked nice. Grey is the colour of horses and greyhounds, she thought. Roger's nose is beginning to turn grey. She heard her mother calling her and, picking up her jacket from the back of the chair, she ran down the stairs for breakfast.

At the cooker, her mum flipped bacon in a pan, while her dad shaved at the sink. "About time!" her mother said. "What are you wearing? Where did you get those trousers from?"

"Tot lent them to me. I like them."

Her mother splashed fat over the eggs. "You look like something out of the poorhouse. Are you allowed to wear those to school?"

Stacey picked up her school bag and took a foil parcel of sandwiches from the kitchen dresser. "They're regulation," she said and let herself out the back door.

* * * * *

She liked the bandages, liked the way they felt on her skin. All wrapped up tight. Like Baby Bunting in a rabbit skin. At bedtime, when she unwound them, her skin looked like tree bark. In the night, her breasts regained their shape, pressing against the fabric of her pyjamas. They felt strange and woke her up. She touched them, held her palms against her nipples. They felt different.

* * * * *

Belinda, her old Walkie-Talkie doll, was the first to go. Stacey dropped her into the roaring garden incinerator. She liked the way the flames made Belinda's face melt into a smooth mask. The fire ate into the plastic, creating a hole where her nose had been. Belinda smelt awful.

Tot sat watching cross-legged on the concrete pathway. "What are you doing . . . David?"

"Burning."

"Why?"

"Because. I don't play with dolls anymore."

A pile of dolls waited on the grass. Baby dolls, crying dolls, all smiling and pink. Barbie rested against the house bricks at the base of the incinerator.

"Can I have your Barbie?" Tot asked.

"No."

"Why not?"

"Because Barbie's all right. I'm keeping Barbie." Stacey undressed Chatty Cathy and dropped her Brownie uniform into the flames.

Tot stared. "You coming out to play later?"

"Can't," Stacey said. "I've got to get ready for Janine's party."

"Can I come?"

"No. It's just family."

Tot twirled her hair around her fingers and sucked at the ends. "David—"

"What?"

"I've got to give Seamus his trousers back."

"Seamus?"

"Yeah. I borrowed them off the O'Flannerys' washing line."

Stacey poked Cathie's head into the flames. Her hair crisped and shrivelled. "All right," she said.

Tot headed up the path towards the alley. She stopped and turned round. "Sorry, David."

Stacey dropped Cathy into the fire and picked up Barbie. "It's not your fault," she said and replaced the lid on the incinerator.

* * * * *

Auntie Norma's girls sat on the floor and played with Janine's birthday present—a padded cosmetics case. Janine had stroked blush on their six-year-old cheeks and painted their eyelids green and blue. Stacey thought they looked frightening, like dwarf clowns, and edged down deeper in the sofa. She was wearing the pink dress and listening to the grown-ups.

Her aunt balanced a teacup in one hand and dabbed a handkerchief to her lips with the other. "Patricia," she said, "your youngest looks like a proper princess! We didn't think Stacey had any legs, did we, girls?" The two little girls pressed their fingers into the pots of colour on the carpet.

Her dad chimed in proudly. "She'll be needing a bra soon. An over-the-shoulder-boulder-holder, won't you, Stace?"

Her mother put her arm protectively around Stacey's shoulders. "Leave her alone, Ted!" She whispered to Norma, "She's at that funny age."

Aunt Norma placed her cup on the tile top coffee table and fiddled with her daughter's plaits. "We've got all that to come, haven't we girls?"

Again, they ignored her, intent on the eye shadow and pencils in Janine's case.

Her aunt leant over and whispered. "Has she started her . . . you-know-what?"

Her mother shook her head and the two women looked rather sadly at Stacey, who looked away and inspected the dents around the sofa's vinyl buttons. How much blood did a rabbit have? A cupful? A jug? How had they got it clean? She looked at her pink dress and counted the stitches in the hem.

Her father reappeared with a six-pack. "I'm just proud of my two girls. Come here, the pair of you and give your old man a hug."

They both stood up and hugged him. Stacey pressed her face against his sweater and smelt faint traces of tobacco and engine oil.

"What more could a man ask for?" he said. "Two beautiful daughters, a lovely wife—"

Aunt Norma piped up from the sofa. "Grandkids?"

He beamed and planted a kiss on Janine's forehead. "A whole football team, eh girls? Five for the Birthday Girl, and six for little Stace, right?"

She disentangled herself from her father's embrace and headed for the kitchen. In search of peanuts, she explained to the room full of family.

* * * * *

In the kitchen, she refilled the peanut bowl and then took the dressmaking shears from the kitchen drawer. She unzipped the dress and stepped out of it. The scissors cut through the shiny fabric like a spade through snow. In minutes, it was a dance of pink streamers on the linoleum. She picked up the bowl of peanuts and, in her vest and knickers, headed back to the front room, where she placed the bowl on the floor next to her cousins.

She sat down on the sofa between her mother and Aunt, scratched at the gusset of her navy blue knickers and picked up the newspaper. "What the fuck's on the telly?" she said, in a ringing imitation of her father's deep voice. "Chuck us a beer, Norma, there's a love!"

Her father burst out laughing. Even Janine stifled a giggle. Her mother, however, did not look impressed and, grabbing her by the arm, propelled her from the room. Aunt Norma dabbed nervously at her lips with a hanky and offered to make everyone a nice pot of tea.

* * * * *

Stacey sat on the toilet seat, a towel around her shoulders like a cape. Tot wielded the dressmaking shears awkwardly, sawing them through hanks of Stacey's yellow hair. "Your mum'll kill you," Tot said.

She sniffed. "She can't kill me twice." She wriggled on the toilet seat. "My bum really, really hurts!"

"Did you actually say the Big Girl's Word?" Tot asked?

"What?"

"The 'F' word."

"Dad does. Mr. O'Flannery does."

"Yeah," Tot replied, "but the 'F' word!"

* * * * *

Stacey liked the feeling of the wind on her neck. It more than made up for the fact that she would never have lacy socks and that her bottom was raw from the hiding her mother had given her. She pushed open the back door. Her mother and Mrs. O'Flannery were drinking tea at the kitchen table.

When she saw Stacey in the doorway, her mother screamed. "Oh my God! What on earth have you done now, child?"

Stacey stood in the doorway and tried to make her voice lower, her shoulders broader. "From now on," she told the two women, "I want to be a boy—"

"Stacey Wright, what the hell have you done to your hair?"

Stacey's voice ramped back up an octave. "No! You've got to call me David from now on."

"David?" Mrs. O'Flannery said, a slight smile lighting around her mouth.

"Yeah, like David Bowie!"

"I'll 'Bowie' you, young lady!" her mother said, flipping at her with a tea towel. "You get to your room right now, and we'll see what your father has to say about all your shenanigans!"

Stacey stormed into the hallway and slammed the kitchen door, just in time to hear Mrs. O'Flannery say she was glad her Lilly was over all this puberty nonsense.

* * * * *

Stacey sat halfway up and halfway down the stairs. In the middle. She could hear her mother sniffling in the kitchen. She could picture her sitting at the Formica table, eyes pink from crying over the hair and the swearing and the fact that her daughter wore trousers and didn't like the pink dress.

Her father understood. He understood about putting her feet in his slippers, about scratching between her legs, and the necessity to be a boy called David. She hadn't actually told him, but she knew he'd understand. After all, there was the pub and the blue smoke and the whippet on the floor. How could he not, she thought, as she cut off Barbie's breasts with the dress-making shears.

* * * * *

In the outside lavatory, a nest of baby spiders was hatching. Stacey sat on the toilet seat and watched them. Hundreds of babies leaving the nest. Hundreds of babies hatching and tumbling down the thick web behind the door.

Something was wrong. Something was different.

She looked down in the pan. The water was pink and swirled. There was blood in the toilet. She had cut her hair, and worn trousers, and burnt her dolls, but there was still blood in the toilet. She pressed her fingers between her legs, trying to stop the flow. She took her hand away and pressed it momentarily against the wall. She left an arc of bloody fingerprints on the whitewash.

* * * * *

Her sister's top drawer was full of bras and knickers. There were also ticket stubs and bundles of letters tied up with rubber bands. There were bath salts and a menu from The Tiger of Bengal restaurant. There was a photo of a boy in a suit. There were no sanitary towels.

As she opened the next drawer down, Janine came into their bedroom, dressed in a bathrobe and rubbing her wet hair with a towel. "What the hell are you doing?" she said. "Get your grubby hands out of my stuff!"

She grabbed Stacey by the shoulder and pulled her backwards. Stacey screamed as her head hit the corner of her bed frame. "You baby!" Janine said. "I didn't hurt you. You fell." She began piling her things back in the top drawer of her chest of drawers. "I've told you about taking my stuff before!" She picked up a cream bra. There was a smear of red on the strap. She glared at Stacey. "You've ruined it, you little cow! Well, you're going to have to pay for a new one now!" She rubbed at the mark. "That's blood!" she said. "How the hell did you get blood on it?"

Stacey didn't answer.

"Oi, I'm talking to you! Are you cut or something?" Janine dropped the bra on the floor. Stacey shook her head. "Oh shit, you haven't been collecting dead birds again, have you?"

"No, I haven't!" said Stacey.

"What then?"

"There's blood in the toilet."

"What?"

"What I said! There's all blood in the toilet."

Janine sat back on her heels. "You've come on? Hell! My little sister!"

"I wanted . . . I don't know what to do. This wasn't meant to happen."

Janine picked up a box of tampons and tossed it across the room. It landed on the bed. "You can borrow some of mine this time. But you'll have to get your own next month."

Stacey read the instructions on the side of the box. She turned to Janine with a look of horror on her face. "I can't do this!"

Janine tapped out one of the tampons and tore the wrapper open. "It's easy," she said. "You just stick this end in and then WHAM! shoot the plunger and Bob's your uncle."

"I can't," she said. "I just CAN'T!"

Janine picked up the tampon from the floor. "I'll get Mum," she said, heading for the door.

"NO! Can you . . . can't you help me?"

Janine looked at Stacey crying on the floor. "Come on," she said, holding out her hand. "And bring the box with you."

* * * * *

Janine shouted over the drone of her hairdryer. "You idiot. Cutting your hair off and wearing trousers isn't going to stop you being a woman. Christ, Stacey, even Billie Jean King has periods!"

"I didn't want . . . I don't want babies and distal-rectomies and . . . and all that blood . . . I thought I—"

Her sister switched off the hairdryer. "Hysterectomy, you mong!" She caught her hair up in a ponytail. "I'm going to have an epidural when I have babies. Or hypnosis." She went cross-eyed in the mirror.

"I don't want babies . . . or boys. It all hurts."

"Doesn't if you go horse riding. Katie said it breaks your hymen."

"What's a hymen?"

Janine rolled her eyes and started to fold laundry, putting it away in her drawers. "For God's sake, cheer up," she said. "It's not the end of the world!" She picked up the gypsy blouse with its row of tin bells and held it out to Stacey.

She looked at the top. It was shirred through with elastic, and embroidered flowers spilled over the shoulders and down the front. Janine shook it at her and all the bells tinkled. "Go on," she said. "Can't have my sister all grown up and looking like a spaz." Janine shook it again. "Go on. You can borrow it . . . but only for today, right?"

* * * * *

The sun fell through the dining room window, picking up the glitter in the pot of eye shadow on the table. Her stomach ached. She felt hot, different. Outside, her father weeded the roses, his back bent over the glossy bushes. She could hear her mother in the kitchen talking to Mrs. O'Flannery about a neighbour whose daughter had run away from home with a representative from the Consideration Insurance Company.

"Hold still!" nagged Janine. "You've got to hold still, or I'll poke you in the eye!"

The eyeliner felt cold against her lid, the foundation heavy on her skin. In the reflection in the window, she looked like Cleopatra. Outside, Roger the dog was digging. Clods of earth rained out from between his legs.

Janine picked up two lipsticks. "Burnished Sunset or Wild Plum?"

She chose Wild Plum and watched as Roger buried Barbie in a hole in front of a clump of dusty lupins.

* * * * *

Stacey took the silver stick of Wild Plum from her jeans pocket and pursed her lips in the mirror above the basins in the Bishop's Croft Community Centre toilets. Rainbow hair slides shimmered in her cropped hair.

Tot sat on the floor and licked her own bare lips. "So there's nothing you can do about it then?"

Stacey glided the lipstick across her lips and then replaced the cap. She slid her lips together and then blotted them on a sheet of toilet paper. "No, absolutely nothing."

"What does it feel like?"

"What?"

"Having a period."

She turned and hopped up onto the counter next to the run of basins. "Like having knives stuck up your . . . vagina."

"Front bottom?"

"It's a vagina. When you have your periods, it's a vagina."

Tot fiddled with the lace on her socks. "Do you think you'll get a flat now?"

"Not yet. Maybe next year though."

Tot stood up and looked at her reflection in the glass. "When you get a flat, can I come and live with you, David?"

"Maybe," she said, checking to be sure the rainbow slides were tightly in place. "But Tot. . . ."

"Yeah?"

"You can't call me David anymore."

Tot looked bewildered. "Well, what can I call you then?"

Stacey tossed the lipstick down to her and watched as she smeared Wild Plum on her lips. "I suppose you better call me Stacey."

My mum cries up the garden behind the shed. She says she's going to check the washing, but that only takes her about a minute. She's hiding behind the shed—I can see bits of her green jumper between the side wall and next door's fence. She's wobbling and when she comes back, her face will be all red and crumpled, like Dad's long johns. I wouldn't cry up there. Too many spiders.

I cry in the bathroom if I can, because it's got a good mirror. I like to watch my face go all blotchy and my eyelashes disappear. Sometimes I try to keep my mouth open while I cry. It's hard.

When Dad left, I had to cry on the landing. Dorothy locked herself in the bathroom and wouldn't come out.

I didn't keep my mouth open. I don't do that anymore.

The Elephant Shaker

Tot peered out from behind the rear bumper of Mr. Patel's Austin Allegro and studied the boys crouched on the pavement outside the Patel house. She took the Stanley Close Spy Club notebook out of her back pocket and began to write. "Saturday 9th October. Michael O'Flannery, Nigel Deepens and Allan Prince sitting on pavement behind Keesal's hedge." She stopped writing and listened.

"My dad says they should all go back on the banana boat," said Michael. "He says they're over here taking our women." He untied the knotted handles of a Sainsbury's carrier bag.

"What women?" Allan asked. "Taking them where?"

Michael shook his head. "Taking them! Having sex with them, you Flid!"

Allan looked confused. "But Mr. Patel's only got one leg."

"What's that got to do with it?"

"I don't know. It just doesn't seem . . . likely. Not with one leg."

Nigel opened the top of the plastic carrier bag and wrinkled his nose. "Stop immigration. Start repatriation. That's what the BNP say. Send all the black bastards home."

"What's repatriation?" asked Allan.

"What Michael said. Sending them back on the banana boat. Here, smell this." Tot watched him push the open carrier bag up into Allan's face. The younger boy shoved it away, covering his nose with his hand. Nigel laughed.

"You bastard!" Allan shouted.

Tot licked the end of her pencil and wrote: "Talking about Keesal and his mum and Dad. Nigel's got a bag of something and is making Allan smell it. Talking about boat full of bananas."

"What's in the bag?" Michael asked.

Allan scooted backwards, away from the bag. "It's shit! It stinks!"

"It's cat shit," said Nigel.

"Why have you got a bag full of cat shit?"

"Whose cat did it?" Allan asked and picked at a scab on his knee.

"It's a little present," Nigel said. "A little housewarming present for our very only Stanley Close Pakis."

Tot frowned and lay down on her front, so she could watch them from under the car. The Deepens boy held the plastic bag in one hand and snaked his way along the pavement and up the Patel's front path. She could hear the squeak of the letterbox as he pushed it open. She watched him empty the bag of cat turds through the opening before he turned and ran back up the path and out across the Green towards the community centre. Michael and Allan scrambled to keep up, their arms and legs pumping like jackhammers, the air full of Allan's high-pitched laughter.

Tot stood up, dropping her pencil and the notepad on the tarmac. The Patel front door slowly opened to frame Keesal and his mother. She stood silent in the doorway, her long black hair loose over her shoulders, and she wore the most beautiful dress Tot had ever seen. She thought the lady was crying.

"Did you see who did this?" Keesal asked.

Tot shook her head, and the pair disappeared back behind the closing door. She picked up the notepad and pencil and rested it on the bonnet of the car. "I don't love Nigel Deepens no more," she wrote, "because he's a Paki basher, and Mr. Patel doesn't even have two legs or anything to fight back with. Mrs. Patel wears beautiful sheets in bright colours. Like pink and lemon. Her dress has lots of little mirrors on it. She looks like a Christmas tree. Keesal looks like Mowgli."

* * * * *

Tot rapped the knocker hard against the front door of number eleven, Stanley Close and stood back on the shiny red brick steps. Mrs. Wright opened the door.

"You want Stacey, dear?" she asked, wiping her floured hands on her apron.

She shook her head. "Is Mr. Wright in?"

The woman smiled and crouched down, so her eyes were level with Tot's. "Isn't he a bit old for you to be playing with?"

"I don't want to play with him," she replied. "I've got to find something out and my dad . . . well, my dad's not here at the moment."

Mrs. Wright smiled sadly, patted Tot on the head, and stepped back into the hallway. "Come on in, sweetheart," she said. "Mr. Wright's in the dining room. Go through."

Tot stepped into a hallway that smelt of jam tarts and furniture polish. Mrs. Wright opened the door into the dining room.

Mr. Wright sat in the corner of the room in front of his engraving machine, hunched over a silver trophy. The whine from the machine was loud and shrill, and the vibrations made the floor tremble beneath her feet. She coughed loudly, but he didn't hear, so she walked across the room and stood at his side. He looked up.

"Hello, dear," he said. "You looking for Stacey?"

She shook her head.

"What then?"

"I've got like a dad question . . . and no Dad." She touched the trophy with her finger. "That's a pretty cup."

He set it on the sideboard and began writing out an invoice on a two-part set. "It's a trophy, Tot. For The Broken Staff. They won the dart league. What did you want to know?"

"What do you call it when someone doesn't like someone, because they don't come from around here?"

"What? Not from Stanley Close?"

"Yeah, but like not from England . . . or even Wales."

"You mean a Scotsman?"

Tot thought about the man in a kilt on the top of the Stanley Close relic tin. She shook her head. "No. When they don't like brown people. Like the Patels."

Mr. Wright stopped filling out the invoice and fiddled with the pen. "Ah, there's lots of names for people like that. Some nice and some not so nice."

"Like Paki basher?"

"Yep, that's one of the not-so-nice ones."

"What's a nice one then? I need a word like they'd use on the nine o'clock news?"

"Well," he said, rubbing his chin, "racist is probably the word you're looking for."

She pulled the notepad from her pocket. "Can you spell that for me, Mr. Wright?"

He spelt it out, and she wrote the word in the book.

"So if someone's a racist, and they put cat shit through someone they don't like's letterbox, what do you call it?"

"I suppose you could call it harassment. That's H-A-R-A-S- S-M-E-N-T." She added it to the page.

He frowned. "Who put cat shit—I mean cat turds—in someone's letter box?

She bit her lip for a moment. "I can't tell you," she said and tapped the cover of the notepad with her pencil. "It's in here now, and you're not a member, so you can't read it. It's a secret thing. Only girls can join." She slipped the book back in her pocket.

* * * * *

The entire chapter of the Stanley Close Spy Club had convened in Tot and Dorothy's garden shed. Tot, recently officially inaugurated, stood fidgeting from foot to foot in the middle of the small, dark hut. Dorothy sat on a deck chair in the shed hunched over the spiral-bound notepad. Lilly, because she was the oldest, had the broken armchair in the corner, and Stacey was perched on the arm of Lilly's chair. Tot had to stand up in the middle, because she was the previous week's spy and had to be debriefed, like James Bond. She kept her eyes focused on her sister, aware that the place was full of spiders and all manner of things that crept and crawled and lived in dark spaces.

Dorothy looked up. "Tot, you've got to tell everyone who you are. It's how we always do it. It's called 'Addressing the Meeting.'"

Tot stood up straight and put her hands on her hips. In a broad Scottish brogue, she said, "My name is Tot. Tot Thompson.—"

Dorothy banged the edge of the notepad on the potting trolley. "Stop with the Bond crap, or I'll revoke your membership!"

"Sorry. I put it all in the book. All the Keesal stuff."

Dorothy turned the pages of the notepad to the end of Tot's report. "You did quite well. Apart from this bit at the end."

"What bit?"

"The bit about Mrs. Patel looking like a Christmas tree, and Keesal being Mowgli."

Lilly leaned forward. "Looked like a what?"

"A Christmas tree."

"She did," said Tot. "She was all glittery and sparkly."

Dorothy tossed the notepad across to Lilly. "I've crossed it out. You can't put things in the Spy Book that aren't facts. And that isn't. Your idea of a Christmas tree and mine might be different."

"What does it matter?" asked Stacey.

Dorothy shifted around in her chair. "Well, imagine if someone needed to kill someone, and the only description the spy gave was that the one who needed to be killed looked like a Christmas tree. Well, it wouldn't help, would it? They might end up killing the wrong person."

Stacey frowned. "But we're not going to kill Mrs. Patel, are we?"

"Of course not! I'm just saying. It's an example. I'm just saying we have to be clear when we spy. It's your turn next week Lilly—"

"But what about Keesal?" Tot said. "What are we going to do about Keesal?"

The girls looked at her. "What do you mean, 'do'?" asked Dorothy.

She checked the floor for bugs and then settled herself down cross-legged. "Stacey's dad said it was harassment and that Nigel was a . . . Lilly, I put it in the book."

Lilly leafed through the notepad. "Racist?"

"Yeah, that's it. We need to do something for Keesal."

Stacey poked Lilly in the ribs and sing-songed, "Tot fancies Keesal! Tot fancies Keesal!"

"I thought she fancied my Nigel," said Lilly, pushing Stacey off the arm. Stacey surfaced from behind the chair, giggling furiously. "Not any more. Tot Patel! Tot Patel!"

Tot half-heartedly threw a seed tray at her, showering dry compost all over Lilly. "Oi! Watch out!" Lilly cried.

"Stop it, everyone!" shouted Dorothy. "It's not up to us to do anything, Tot. We just spy on people."

"We could spy on Nigel and Michael," Tot said. "We could all spy on them and then tell their mums and dads what they do!" She smiled at her bright idea.

"No way! That's informing, and I'm not a dirty, rotten tea leaf!"said Lilly. She brushed specks of compost off her shoulders. "Anyway, my dad says Mr. Powell had the right idea and that there's going to be roads of blood 'n gore all over the place if they keep letting immigrants in."

"It's not tea leaf," said Dorothy. "It's squealer. Tealeafs are thiefs."

"I'm not going to do either of them," Lilly said.

"You just don't want us spying on you and Nigel kissing again!" Stacey sat down next to Tot on the floor. "Anyway, it's rivers of blood. Mr. Powell's a spigot. My dad said so. Keesal's just as English as we are."

"Bigot, you Wally!" Dorothy said.

"I'm not English. I'm Irish," said Lilly, "and he's a dirty Paki!"

"My Dad's not a dirty Paki!"

"No, Keesal's a Paki, you spaz!"

Tot stood up. "Keesal is not a Paki. His Dad's from Calcutta and that's India!"

Lilly laughed. "He's still a Paki. It's the same thing."

"How would you like it if they put cat shit in your letterbox?" Tot asked.

"My dad would kick their arses!" Lilly said. "Anyway, they're taking a house off a white family who needs it. They should stay where they came from. Or in Towford. Or London." Lilly grabbed a ball of twine from the shelf over the chair and threw it up in the air chanting, "Keesal's a monkey! Keesal's a monkey!"

Tot couldn't believe it. Dorothy sat there saying nothing, and Lilly kept chanting, all the time laughing and throwing the ball of string in the air. Even Stacey didn't seem to know what to do—she sat studying the end of her shoe and poking the pointed end of the bulb dibber into the floor.

Tot picked up a clay pot from the stack behind the door, ignoring the webs and the spiders that scattered as the pile fell over. "Take that back!" Lilly just laughed. Tot turned to her sister. "Dorothy, make her take it back!" Dorothy fiddled with the hem of her dress. All Tot could hear was the sound of the ball of twine in Lilly's hands and her chanting.

Tot slowly drew her arm back, the clay pot heavy in her hand. "Lilly, PLEASE take it back!" She was close to crying. It felt as if everything was about to unravel. The summer was over, and it was meant to have ended differently. They were a team. The Stanley Close Spy Club. But now it was just her and three other girls in a shed full of summer leftovers and spiders and silverfish. And her dad had gone to America. She threw the terra-cotta pot, and it hit Lilly in the middle of her forehead. It shattered into large shards that landed in Lilly's lap.

The shed was silent. The three girls watched as blood trickled down from a gash in Lilly's blonde hairline. The red mixed with her yellow hair and slowly Lilly touched her head. She stared at the blood on her fingers and then back at Tot. Tot knew she should run, but she couldn't. It had to end now—here in her Dad's potting shed. Running would only make it worse.

"You bloody little cow! I'll fucking kill you!" Lilly threw herself on Tot, windmilling her arms, hands bunched into fists and heaping blow upon blow on Tot's head and shoulders. Dorothy launched out of the chair and pulled Lilly off, the pair of them landing in a heap back in the armchair. The old ratty chair overturned and spilled them both out onto the sacks of last year's bulbs.

Stacey grabbed Tot's arm and dragged her from the shed. Over her shoulder, she shouted at Lilly, "and you're a bloody thick Irish Mick, who ought to go home with the bananas in a boat!"

Tot began to cry.

* * * * *

The two girls sat in the space behind the sofa in Stacey's front room cutting out their favourite outfits from the Kay's catalogue. Stacey still had soil in her hair.

"Thanks, Stacey," said Tot.

"S'alright. Are you okay?"

Tot nodded. "Stacey?"

"Yeah?"

"Did you really do it with your cousin?"

"Nah, course I didn't." She pulled a large clump of potting compost out from her plaits.

"Why did you say it, then?"

"I was angry with Dorothy. Having all the good things to spy about. She always gets the good things."

"She cries a lot though," Tot picked another lump of potting compost from Stacey's hair.

"Why?"

"I don't know. Mum says it's her age." Tot turned the catalogue page. "Will you start crying now you have periods?"

"Yeah, I suppose so. Did Mrs. Patel's dress really have little mirrors in it?" Stacey carefully snipped around a pair of three-tone suede shoes with real stacked heels.

"Yeah," Tot said. "It was the most beautiful sheet I've ever seen."

"They call them saris. My mum said."

"I want one," Tot said, cutting round a cheesecloth blouse.

"If you marry Keesal, you'll have loads of them."

"I'm not going to marry him."

"Kiss him then," said Stacey, placing the shoes in a paper bag marked *Christmas 1972*.

"I'm not going to kiss him!" Tot said, grabbing the paper shoes out of the bag and snipping them in half.

"You pig!" shrieked Stacey, ripping the paper blouse in two and giggling.

"Fainites!" Tot screamed, crossing her fingers and holding them above her head. "Fainites! You can't rip no more!" The two girls, screaming with laughter, scrambled to protect their paper clothes collections. Tot covered hers with her hands, her fingers still crossed.

Truce established, they sat back against the wall and sipped at their drinks.

Stacey sighed loudly. "Oh, Tot! I called Lilly a thick Irish Mick!"

"That's nothing. I threw a flower pot at her!"

"Do you think we're out of the Club?"

She looked at Stacey. "I don't care. She deserved it anyway. Keesal's not a monkey!"

"No," Stacey said, carefully edging her paper bag of cut-out clothes under the sofa. "He's a Mowgli!" They again collapsed into a heap of giggles.

"Have you ever been in his house?" whispered Stacey when she got her breath back.

"Nah. But he said I could go round for my tea."

"I wouldn't want tea. Their house smells."

"It doesn't!"

"It does. It smells of curry."

"That's a nice smell."

"Still smells." Stacey carefully lifted a chocolate Jaffa Cake from the plate of biscuits. "They don't have salt and pepper in their house," she said, holding the biscuit in her hand, like a squirrel with a nut, and nibbled around the flattened outside rim.

"What do they have, then?"

"Garam stuff. Like curry powder."

"They do have salt and pepper! You can't have curry powder on chips."

Stacey stuffed the rest of the biscuit in her mouth. "I bet his walls are pink . . . "

"with lime green carpets . . . "

"and a gold tablecloth . . . "

"and snakes in baskets."

"Snakes?" asked Stacey.

"Yeah," Tot said, finishing her orange. "Keesal's dad's a snake charmer. Like Labi Sifri. He sits cross-legged on a silver cushion and charms cobras out of their laundry basket."

"He can't."

"He can," said Tot. "I've heard him play the flute."

"No, I mean sit with his legs crossed. He's only got one leg."

"Maybe he sits on a chair then."

* * * * *

Tot held the year's last blooming rose between her fingers and snipped off its head. She pulled away the petals and dropped them into the Tupperware box on the path. Rose petals and laburnum and privet leaves. She wanted eucalyptus, but the tree was outside the kitchen window, and her mother was in there cooking dinner. She had to make do with privet. She shook the box and inhaled. It smelt pungent and warm. She snapped the lid in place and headed for Keesal's house.

She paused at the top of the pathway. The front room curtains were closed and Mr. Patel's car was gone. She walked on tiptoe to the front door and pulled the lid off the plastic box, setting it on the ledge where Mrs. Patel put her empty milk bottles. She took a handful of the warm petals and leaves and emptied it through the letterbox. When she was halfway through posting the fourth handful, the door opened.

As it swung back, her hand became trapped in the metal slot, and she was forced to lurch inside the hallway. Keesal stared at her and then at the crushed flowers in a pile on the Welcome doormat. She pulled her hand from the letterbox, reached back out to the milk bottle ledge, and retrieved the Tupperware container.

"Hold your hands out," she said. He did, and she emptied the remainder of the petals into his upturned palms.

"What's this for?" he asked, peering at the flowers in his hands.

"Nice things in your letterbox," she replied. "To cancel out the cat shit. Right?"

He stood mute, puzzled at the rose petals, laburnum, and privet leaves. She tried to explain again.

"It's like, let's say, if you fall off your bike when you're opposite the sweetshop. Then for weeks and weeks, each time you go past, you think you're going to fall off again? Yeah?"

He dropped the petals to the floor. "Er, yeah, I think so."

"Well, that's because you think the sweetshop and your falling off is, like, part of the same thing. Sweetshop equals fall off. Or letterbox equals cat shit. So now, you've got letterbox equals flowers. S'nicer, isn't it?"

"Er, yeah. Thanks," he said, slowly closing the door.

"Any time, Keesal. Anytime."

* * * * *

Tot slid the thick shard of hopscotch slate around the palm of her hand three times for luck. She was on number nine and for some reason, throwing onto number nine always gave her trouble. Ten was fine and King and Queen were easy, even though they were furthest away. It was just number nine that was a bugger. She threw the slate, and it landed bang in the centre of the paving slab chalked with a rounded nine. It was sliding the slate around her palm that did it. She saved that magic for hard things. It didn't always work.

Mr. Damson stood on the other side of the hedge, giving the privet its final trim of the year. She always played hopscotch here because the Damsons had the best bit of pavement—no cracks.

He stopped clipping and passed her a broom over the hedge. "Sweep up those leaves, there's a good girl."

She took the wide-headed broom and swept the privet clippings into a pile at the end of the path where Mr. Damson scooped them up and dropped them onto the heap of leaves in the wheelbarrow.

"Just your mother's turrets to go, and then we can dump all this." He picked up the shears again and began trimming the topiary turrets at either end of the Thompson's hedge. She jumped and then hopped onto number eight, stood on one leg to retrieve her slate, and then jumped onto the King and Queen.

Mr. Patel was also outside on the pavement trimming his own hedge. Keesal followed behind him, picking up the snipped privet leaves. She waved, but Mr. Patel ignored her and walked into his front garden, his artificial foot knocking unevenly on the rough concrete path. Tot and Keesal shrugged at each other. She jumped around and hopped and skipped back to the wheelbarrow into which Mr. Damson was loading the last few leaves.

"Jump in then, Miss Thompson!" he said. She slipped the slate into her pocket and leapt into the pile of leaves. Mr. Damson began to push the barrow up the road.

"You want a ride, Keesal?" she called as they trundled past. Mr. Patel looked doubtfully over the hedge.

"Don't worry," she said to the one-legged Indian man, "Mr. Damson here used to live in a posh house, and I'm only eight. We're not racists!"

Keesal looked at his father, who nodded, then continued to snip away at his hedge.

"Can you wait just a minute? I want to get something." Keesal rushed down the alley and disappeared behind the back gate.

Mr. Damson smiled politely at Mr. Patel over the hedge, and Tot knelt up in the barrow, so she could see over into Keesal's front garden. Mr. Patel clipped tiny snips from his side of the privet hedge. Tot watched his leg. Mr. Damson coughed and then began to whistle softly.

"Mr. Patel," Tot said. The Indian man looked up, still clipping at the air. "Was it a shark?" He frowned. "Or a tiger? I've heard tigers can be terribly fierce if you cut their jungles down." She leaned a little further over the hedge. "Is it wooden or plastic?"

Mr. Patel stared at Tot, who knelt in the leaves and waited expectantly for an answer. He put the clippers down on the grass and walked out from behind the hedge onto the pavement. "Good day, Mr. Damson," he said. His accent was precise and careful. He tugged up his trousers at the knee and exposed a shiny shin the colour of bubble gum. Hubba Bubba bubble gum. "Would you like to touch it, little girl?" He walked towards the barrow, his foot rasping slightly on the pavement. Tot panicked at the pink plastic and fell back in the barrow. Both Mr. Damson and Mr. Patel laughed, a slightly embarrassed yet friendly laugh.

Keesal came dashing out of the back gate and jumped into the wheelbarrow next to Tot. Grunting, Mr. Damson lifted the handles once again, said goodbye to Mr. Patel, and steered the barrow to the top of the road, where a mud track led off between the houses down towards the copse.

Tot could feel Keesal's shoulder pressing against her own. The rusty lip of the wheelbarrow cut into her back, and the sharp green smell of the privet clippings was overpowering.

Ahead, the oak trees marked the spot where all the fathers brought their clippings at the weekend. Small piles of leaves dotted the verge, left like scent markers throughout the summer, each pile pungent and obvious. Mr. Damson slowed the wheelbarrow.

"Ready, you two?" he asked. They nodded and he upended the barrow, emptying the leaves and the two giggling children onto the verge. He turned and started back up the mud track towards Stanley Close.

Keesal sat up and fished around in his trouser pocket. He pulled out something pink and lime green and placed it in Tot's hand.

"For you," he said. "Don't tell anyone, though!"

She opened her fingers and there in her palm was a china Indian elephant. Its pink and green howdah was pierced with holes and when she upended it, her palm filled with pepper. She tasted it. It was woodsmoke, a bonfire on her tongue.

WINTER 1972

There's a fossil on one of the cobblestones outside the post office. It's an echinoderm—my dad told me. He said they lived in the sea hundreds and hundreds of years ago.

So it's dead.

But instead of being buried in the sand and having blue and green fishes and octopuses and sea horses to keep it company, it has to sit on that cobble in the rain and the snow. Boys on bikes run over it and dogs piddle on it. One day, it had a big glob of bubble gum stuck to it.

Before I go over to the shops to get my saving stamp on a Saturday morning, I put a sprinkle of salt and some water in a cup and take it with me. I pour it over the tiny echinoderm until she glistens.

I've tried to dig her out, but the cobble's set in concrete. It's sad when something's stuck in the wrong place.

The Piano Lesson

❊

Tot swung on the newel post at the top of the staircase, eavesdropping on her sister, who was having yet another telephone argument with her boyfriend. He didn't come round to the house anymore, but she called him most evenings. The calls seemed to consist of long stretches of silence interspersed with short chops of angry argument. Dorothy turned to the wall, the receiver cradled under her chin. Tot could tell she was crying from the way her shoulders jumped.

She slouched down the steps, sidled past her sister, and crawled into the space between the shoe cupboard and the coat rack below the stairs. She dragged the yellow, blue, and red box of fireworks from the corner behind all the coat hems and umbrellas and opened the lid. Lined up in cardboard separators were rockets, catherine wheels, roman candles, and exploding jacks. And a paper roll of sparklers. She sniffed the long grease-proof roll. It smelt dry. It smelt like lead pencils. She took a rocket from one of the slots, replaced the lid, and slid the box back behind the hanging coats.

At the kitchen sink, Tot picked up a rinsed milk bottle and stuck the rocket inside, its blue flash paper trailing down the neck, the crisp blue deepening and softening against the wet glass. She quietly placed the bottle on the kitchen table next to where her mother sat reading through a pile of government pamphlets about child support and free school dinners.

"Mum?"

"What, Tot? I'm busy."

"Are we having fireworks?"

Her mother pushed away the pamphlet and rubbed her eyes. "No, not tonight. I'm too tired to sort it all out."

Tot jiggled the bottle. "But it's November 5th. Dad always does fireworks on Guy Fawkes Night."

Her mother grabbed up the bottle and slammed it down on the opposite side of the table. "Yes, well, that was then, and this is now. If your father hadn't walked out on us, we'd do fireworks. But he did, so we won't."

Tot reached over and retrieved the rocket from the bottle. It hung from her hand like a empty gun.

Her mother looked down at the rocket. She sighed and, shaking her head, wrapped her arms around her youngest daughter. "Oh, come here," she said, stroking her hair and kissing her forehead. "We went to the display up the park last night, didn't we?"

"So why did we get a box of fireworks if we're not having any?"

"I didn't 'get' them. They were left. On the doorstep." Her mother pulled open the drawer beneath the table and brought out three pairs of gaudy pink and green mittens. "One of the neighbours left them on the step with these."

"Can I have a pair?"

Her mother placed all three pairs next to the milkbottle. "Help yourself," she said, and blew her nose on the last sheet from a roll of toilet paper. "I've got too much to do, sweetheart, to think about fireworks. Why don't you go and practice your piano?"

Tot slipped on the mittens and wandered into the dining room. She sat down on the padded bench seat and began to pick her way through "Chopsticks" using just her mittened thumbs. In the light from the lamppost at the end of the path, she could make out Mr. Damson's bicycle propped up against the dustbin in their alleyway next door.

She went back to the kitchen and pulled two fresh toilet rolls from the cupboard under the sink. She handed one to her mother and stuck the other under her arm. "If we're not having fireworks," she said, "can I go and see Mr. Damson?"

"Why would you want to go and see Mr. Damson?"

"He needs a piano teacher."

"You are the strangest child, Tot." Her mother pulled a sheet from the toilet roll and blew her nose. "Alright then . . . as long as you don't bother him too much."

She pocketed her mother's felt-tip freezer pen from the organizer on the fridge door and wandered back into the hall, where she handed the other toilet roll to her sister. Dorothy pulled a sheet off the roll. Her crying had reached the gulping stage, and Tot knew the ritual slamming down of the telephone was just seconds away. She didn't like how he made her sister cry all the time.

She retrieved her jacket from its hook under the stairs, then collected two oranges from the fruit bowl on the hall table. She dropped the fruit into her jacket pocket. "Bye, Dorothy," she said, before doubling back and grabbing the telephone from her sister's hand. "YOU'RE A BLOODY BUGGER, CHRISTO-PHER TENDALL!" she shouted into the receiver, then dashed out the front door before her sister could complain.

She walked up the pathway to the Damsons' front door. The bicycle was there, but the house was in darkness. She stood on tiptoe on the bottom doorstep to peer through the high bay window into the Damsons' living room. She couldn't see much because the windows were grimy, but she could make out the large television set, quiet and grey in the corner of the room. And a picture. A huge picture in a chunky gold frame hung over the fireplace. She rubbed at the window, but the dirt was on the inside of the glass.

The front door swung open, and Mr. Damson stepped out onto the doorstep clutching two empty milk bottles. "And what are you doing peering in my window, Little Miss Thompson?" He set the milk bottles in the plastic holder on the top step.

Tot slipped on the damp step and banged her chin on the windowsill. "Bugger!" she said, holding her chin with one hand and sticking the other out towards Mr. Damson. "Hello, Mr. Angelfish."

He took her hand and gently shook it. "It's Mr. Damson. You can drop the Angelfish now."

"Deal," she said.

"So, why were you peering through my window?"

She edged past him into the hallway. "I thought it was about time for that piano lesson I promised you," she said. "But if you had been watching *Horizon*, I was going to come back later. My dad watches . . . my dad always watched it and, well . . . we weren't allowed to disturb him when he was watching the telly." She opened the door to the front room. "Wow," she said, "that's not real gold around that picture, is it?"

Mr. Damson followed her in. "No, it's gilt," he said. "Gilt over plaster."

"Oh, bummer! What's the picture meant to be, anyway?"

"It's an abstract."

"Yeah, but what's it meant to be?"

"It's Duchamp's *Nude Descending a Staircase*."

She studied the picture from the doorway. Then she sat down on the spindly chintz sofa and looked at it some more. "A lady with no clothes on?"

Mr. Damson nodded.

"Descending a stairway?"

He nodded again.

"That means going down, right?"

"Yes."

"Where's her legs?" she asked, cocking her head.

"Wherever you want them to be, I suppose."

Tot looked up at him sadly. "I've got a proper picture at home. It's dolphins. Paint-by-Numbers." She stood up and grabbed his hand. "You can have it if you like."

He chuckled.

"Come on, then," she said. "Where's the piano?"

"Through here." He opened the door that led into the dining room, where Mrs. Damson sat at the table in the window reading a magazine.

"We have a visitor, Pamela," he said.

Tot stuck out her hand again. "Tot Thompson," she said. "From next door."

"Pleased to meet you," said Mrs. Damson, shaking her hand.

"Miss Thompson's here to teach me how to play the piano," Mr. Damson said. "Would you like a cup of tea, Tot? We were just about to have one."

She nodded, sat down on the straight-back chair at the piano, and pulled off her mittens. She dropped them to the floor and flexed her fingers before raising the rosewood lid. "Wow!" she said. "This is a Chappel!" She looked up at the pair of them. "You must have been really rich before you lost all your money!"

* * * * *

"Stick your hands out," she said, and Mr. Damson obediently spread his hands, palm down, on his knees. Tot pulled the felt-tip pen from her pocket, uncapped it, and began to number his fingers. She wrote "1" on each thumb, "2" on his index fingers, ending up with each little finger labelled with a neat "5."

"Now, turn your hands over as if you're holding something."

He turned over his hands. She pulled the oranges from her pockets and placed one in each of his palms. "Don't grab at them!" she said. "Just let them lay there for a minute." He sat holding the oranges while she wrote "C" on an ivory key in the middle of the keyboard. He winced.

Tot looked up. "Oh, don't you worry. Look, it comes off." She spat on her finger and rubbed at the key, spreading black ink across the ivory. "Oh . . . well, nearly." Tot scooted round on the chair. "You got any Ajax, Mrs. Damson?"

"No!" said Mr. Damson, still holding the oranges. "It'll be fine. Just fine."

"Anyway," she said, taking the oranges and putting them in her lap, "let's get on with it. Keep your hands in that shape, but turn them over."

He did. She gently took his thumbs and placed his left in the middle of the inky piano key and his right below on the edge. "That's middle C," she said. "It's the biggest, most important key in the whole piano world. You've got to remember that." He nodded. "Now, press down." The round sound of middle C resonated above the piano. "You've just played middle C. Easy, isn't it?"

Mrs. Damson returned with a tray and passed around the tea before returning to her magazine. Tot took a sip, then gently dribbled it back into the cup. "There's no milk," she said. "No, don't get up. I'll go and get some."

She came back from the kitchen with a bottle of milk and a bag of sugar. She slurped milk into her cup and fished out the wedge of lemon.

"My sister—she's fourteen, fifteen in January—she puts lemon in her tea. She bought some Earl Grey and Orange Pekoe from Habitat because she thinks it's swanky. I like PG Tips with milk. Sugar, Mr. Damson?" He shook his head. "Right then. Hit the key next to middle C with your right hand number two. That's your pointy finger." He did. "Now the next one with number three." And so on, until he had played the entire five-finger scale in the key of C major. When he had mastered that, she made him invert the scale by playing it with his left hand. For the next five minutes, the room was full of the sound of miss-hit keys, Tot shouting numbers and Mr. Damson laughing. Even Mrs. Damson smiled, before retiring to the peace of the kitchen to finish her magazine.

"Enough!" he said, standing up and stretching. "My fingers are tired, Tot. I need a break!"

"Alright," she said, lowering the piano lid. "I can't teach you any more yet anyway. I've only got this far myself." She finished her tea. "But I can come back and show you some more next week?"

"That would be great. I'll look forward to it."

She took one of the oranges from her lap and handed it to Mr. Damson. "Why didn't you play this piano when you lived in your big house?"

"It was my mother's. She lived with us, but she didn't like anyone else touching her piano."

"Why?" She pulled the peel from her own orange in one piece and hung it over the top of her ear.

He laughed. "I suppose because she was worried we might damage it."

She eased a segment off the orange and popped it in her mouth, chewing thoughtfully. "So she played piano, and you and Mrs. Damson listened?"

"Yes," he replied, trying to peel his own orange in one continuous spiral.

"So no one ever played piano to your mum then?"

"No, I suppose no one did."

"Sad. Was it lovely being rich?"

"Yes, Tot. It was very lovely."

"What was the best bit?"

"Oh, I don't know. Not worrying about money, I suppose. And we had two cars. And I had a big company where people made things for hospitals."

"We haven't got a lot of money. We've got more than the O'Flannerys at number seven. But we're not rich. Did you play polo like Prince Charles?"

"Er, no. We weren't that rich. But I did have a hobby."

"Yeah?"

"Yes. I collected fishing reels."

"What's a fishing reel?"

Mr. Damson stood up and picked a wooden reel from the bookcase by the window and handed it to Tot. The wood was the colour of conkers, but swirled with black and orange.

"Gosh," she said. "That's beautiful. Did you catch many fish with it?" She jiggled her head, and her orange peel earring bobbled against her thin neck.

He took the reel back and rubbed it against the front of his cardigan. "No, I never fished, Tot. I just collected the reels."

Outside, she could hear fireworks exploding above the house. "I bet you went on a lot of holidays. I bet you had a holiday every month or something."

He laughed. "Not quite, but we did go away every year."

"Did you go to Clacton-on-Sea? I love Clacton. The sand at the back of the beach is too dry to dig in. It's like salt and it's full of fag ends, but down by the waves, it's lovely. The sand's squishy, like toothpaste. It's great for holes."

"No, never been to Clacton. We used to go to France. The Dordogne."

"We go to Clacton on the coach. My dad . . . my dad used to play trumpet at The Eagle and every year, we went to Clacton with all the people from the pub. Uncle Jimmy and Aunty Carol. . . . " She stopped and took the orange peel from her ear. She fiddled with it and then dropped it in her pocket.

"That sounds fun." He coiled his single piece of peel on the top of the piano and pulled off a segment of orange.

"Anyway, for dinner, we'd go to the fish and chip shop, and they all have proper dinners, like cod and chips and mushy peas. But I just have bread and chips—because I was on holiday, and you're allowed to do that when you're on your holidays. Do you like chip butties, Mr. Damson?"

"I don't think I've had one."

She looked at him in amazement. "What, never?"

"No, never."

"So you've never lined up all your chips on a slice of bread and butter and then jammed another slice on top and mushed it down with your hand and eaten it?"

"No, I don't believe I ever have."

She shook her head. "Mr. Damson, I hope you don't mind me saying this, but I think it's a good thing you've come to live in Stanley Close. I mean, what with the picture and not fishing and never having been to Clacton on a coach and butties and everything . . . you've got to start doing some proper things!" She slipped off the seat. "I'll be back in a minute." She slid her chair back under the dining room table.

Mr. Damson picked up his coil of orange peel from the top of the piano and hung it over his left ear. "Things like this?" he said.

"Yeah." Tot fished in her pocket and hung her orange peel back over her ear. "Things just like that."

* * * * *

Mrs. Damson reappeared in the dining room with a plate of chocolate biscuits and set it on top of the piano.

"Has Tot gone?" she asked.

Mr. Damson shook his head. "No. She's just gone to . . . oh, I don't know. She said she'd be back in a minute."

"Funny little thing, isn't she," she said. "Why have you got orange peel hooked over your ear?"

He held his hands out in front of him and inspected the numbers written on his fingers. "Apparently, this is all you need to know in order to successfully play five-finger scales in C Major. To think we had this piano for all those years, and I didn't even know where middle C was." He lifted the piano lid. "It's right there, you know. Just underneath the name plate." He pointed to it, and she nodded. "They do that so you can find it easily. Imagine that."

She picked up a biscuit and turned it over and over between her fingers. He reached across and covered her hand with his. "Are you going to leave me, Pamela?"

She stared at him. "You silly man! What on earth makes you ask that?"

"Oh, I don't know. Me losing the house and everything. Having to move here. I wouldn't blame you, you know."

She broke the biscuit in two and handed him half. He began to slowly nibble around the edges, then crammed it all in his mouth at once. "Tot feels sorry for me, because I've never been to Clacton . . . or had a chip butty."

"Clacton? Didn't you have an aunt who lived there?"

"Yes. Never visited though. Especially not on a coach, and Tot reckons that's the only way."

"She's eight years old, Gerald."

"Yes, she's eight-years old, but she's got a way of looking at things that. . . ."

They heard the kitchen door creak open and then slam shut. "Yooey!" Tot called. "I'm back!"

* * * * *

Tot propped the painting of the leaping dolphins against the side of the piano and grabbed Mr. and Mrs. Damson by the hands. "Come outside! Quick!" She pulled them through the tiny kitchen, out the back door, down the alley, and into the small back garden. She pointed to the sky over the rubbish dump. "Listen!" A tinny whine became louder and stronger, until it shrieked into the roaring whoosh of a rocket that exploded into five bouquets of red and yellow fire flowers.

"Bloody brilliant!" Tot said and pulled a long greaseproof package from her pocket. She ripped open the top with her teeth and handed each of them a sparkler. "I'm not allowed to do this bit," she said and gave a box of matches to Mr. Damson. "These are sparklers, and you light them, and then it's like having a magic wand with fizz coming out the end. You can write things or draw love hearts on the sky."

He struck a match and lit the end of the sparklers, each erupting into brilliant liquid stars that dripped from the ends of the wires. Pamela slipped her hand in his, he put his arm around Tot's shoulder, and the three of them wrote their wishes on the night, the traces of all their dreams spelt out in the dark for one luminous second, before fading from sight.

My dad told me swans marry for life. He said if one of the swans flies away, the other dies of a broken heart.

There was a swan on the canal last week. All on her own. She was kissing her reflection. I threw her bread, but she just kept kissing and kissing and kissing. She didn't even notice I was there.

On Animal Magic, a lady swan said she'd got 25,000 feathers, and that a man is called a cob and a lady is called a pen. Baby swans—cygnets—are grey and then they go brown and then they go white. They can't bite, but they can break your leg or your arm with just one blow of their wings.

I know it's really an actress speaking—I'm not a complete spaz. She said in a quacky voice that swans DON'T marry for life. She said it was a FALLACY, and that they can have lots of husbands and wives. Sometimes even four.

My Dad's a swan—a shitty, smelly, lying swan with flat orange feet and pondweed up his bum. I hope he swallows a fishing line in his big fat beak and gets lead poisoning. I hope the Queen eats him for Christmas dinner.

The Gate Crasher

✳

Tot pleated the pink paper serviette lengthways as her mother had shown her and secured it across the centre with a tight loop of wire. She watched her mother across the table. Each time their gazes met, her mother smiled the kind of smile puppets wear. A Jack-in-the-Box smile. Now you see it, now you don't.

The dining room door was open. Through the front room windows, she could just make out Mr. O'Flannery's dilapidated yellow van in the Community Centre car park. She'd heard Uncle Ernie say the O'Flannerys were doing the bar for the Residents' Association Christmas party that night. She'd also heard him say that he gave Sean O'Flannery until about nine o'clock before he'd drunk all the Association's profits and collapsed on the floor. She liked Uncle Ernie. They made each other laugh.

"Come on," her mother said. "We've got another thirty of these to make before I go over and decorate the tables." She slid another packet of serviettes across the table, picked up one of Tot's pleated sets, and fanned out each end so that the bundle opened out into a circle. She slipped a red-lacquered nail in between the piles of tissue and gently teased up each layer, one after the other. In less than a minute, a pink paper carnation bloomed in her palm.

Tot ripped open the cellophone package, placed four of the serviettes on top of each other, and began pleating again. Over. Fold. Turn. Over. Fold. Turn.

"Mum?"

"What?"

"Will Santa be coming to our house this year?"

"What's made you start believing in Santa all of a sudden?" Her mother reached for another wired serviette set.

"I thought . . . what with dad not being here, maybe Santa would bring us presents instead." Tot picked up a length of wire and looped it around the middle of the pleated tissue.

Her mother poured a splash of crimson ink into a saucer. "There'll be presents. I'm not sure what, but there will be presents. You've just got to be a good girl for another couple of weeks."

Tot continued folding and turning.

In the living room, Uncle Ernie was hanging Christmas decorations. Twisted blue and silver garlands ran from the corners of the room and clustered at the central light fitting. She watched him balance precariously on the old wooden stepladder that rested against the chimney breast. He was singing and talking to himself all at the same time.

"*I'm dreaming* . . . there we go . . . one more twist . . . *of a white Christmas!*"

She watched him climb down the ladder. Silver Lametta strips hung over his shoulder, and he clutched two of Grandma's old paper Chinese lanterns in his hand.

Her mother rapped the table. "Come on, Dreamer! Get folding." She dipped the tips of the paper flower in the saucer. The crimson liquid crept up the tissue petals.

"Where's Dorothy?" Tot asked. "And why isn't she helping?"

* * * * *

Lilly O'Flannery was fed up having a retard for a brother. He'd lost his best trousers and then managed to put his jacket on backwards. Her mother said if they wanted to go to the party, Lilly would have to sort him out. After all, she had more than enough to do setting up the bar.

Lilly sat him down on the edge of her bed and tried to tug off his jacket. Seamus wriggled and smiled a big gappy smile.

"'Unnnnneeeee!' 'Unnnnneeeee!" he giggled.

"It is not funny, Seamus O'Flannery, and stop sticking your arms out like that!"

He could never keep spit safely in his mouth when he laughed, and a big glob dropped onto the sleeve of the jacket.

"Now look what you've gone and done, you loon!" she cried, wiping his sleeve on the bedspread. His smile descended into a wail, his huge blank eyes filling with tears.

"Oh Sweet Jesus, here we go," she said as he burrowed into her pillows like a small rodent, his sobs and wails rising and falling like a siren. She grabbed his skinny shoulders and held him tight to her chest.

"It's okay, Chickie," she crooned into his ear. "Lilly didn't mean it. Bad Lilly!" She picked a stray feather that had escaped the pillow's striped ticking. "Here! A feather, Seamie! A magic feather!" She handed him the curled brown wisp. He tested it on his lips first and then on the tip of his nose. He smiled and trailed it around the rim of his ear.

"Fevvvver," he said. "Fevvvver." He smiled and let her take off his jacket and slip it on the right way around.

Her mother shouted up the stairs. "Have you found your brother's trousers yet?"

"Oh, for God's sake, give me a blessed minute, would you?"

"I'll give you a blessed slap on the arse if you cheek me again. FIND HIS TROUSERS! And Lilly—"

"What"

"Don't forget to bring that box of Babycham glasses over. I can't carry them, and your father's got the van."

"Okay."

"And Lilly—"

"WHAT!"

"Make sure your brothers are clean and tidy before you bring them over to the party. And watch the cleavage—"

"OKAY!"

Lilly turned back to her brother and wondered how he had managed to lose his only pair of good trousers. He sat on the edge of the bed in his underpants, socks, and jacket, tickling his eyebrow with the feather. He giggled, a wide, wet smile on his lips, and offered the feather to Lilly. She thought about Dorothy. "Aw, Seamus," she said, hugging him again. "Sometimes, there's just not enough feathers to go around."

She took the feather and poked it in her pocket. Where the hell could he have lost his trousers, she wondered. Maybe they were at the back of the airing cupboard? As she made for the door, she saw a light flickering in the darkness beyond her bedroom window. It was coming from the direction of the abandoned Stanley Close Spy Club. Someone was out there with a torch.

* * * * *

The kitchen at number fourteen was full of steam. Mrs. Wright's laundry copper sat on the back ring bubbling and clanking with a full load of eggs. Stacey watched her dip in a slotted spoon and draw one out. Her mother held it up to the light from the window, the water on the shell evaporating in seconds.

"That's done," her mother said, wiping her forehead with her apron. She slid the copper off the ring and across to the drainer where she upended it into the sink. Four dozen eggs landed with a brittle thud. "Remind me never to offer to boil eggs again."

"Or do these rotten crackers." Stacey looked down at the rows of Ritz lined up on the kitchen table. The greasy-handled knife slipped from her fingers and fell to the floor.

"Aw, Stacey! You're meant to put a squirt of cheese and THEN a triangle of cucumber on those crackers. Not the other way around!" Her mother took out a marble pastry slab from the cupboard under the sink and cleared room for it on the draining board.

Stacey dipped under the table to retrieve the knife, which was covered in dog hair. She wiped it on the tablecloth. She was sick of crackers, and her finger hurt from squeezing the cheese spread tubes. It seemed like she'd been squeezing and spreading all day.

"How many crackers can Stanley Close eat?" she said, throwing the crumpled tube into the bin by the back door and taking a new one from the box on the table.

"If we went by your appetite, Little Miss Greedy Gannet, we'd be here spreading until midnight." Her mother filled the sink with cold water and tipped in a bowl of ice cubes. "Come on. Chop chop! Mrs. Damson's coming over at five for those. And I've got to devill these damned eggs yet."

Stacey squeezed cheese onto another cracker and pictured her Christmas dress on its hanger in her bedroom. They had picked it up the previous weekend at Wembley Market. It was beautiful and had cost a fortune. She remembered her mother handing over the five-pound note. The market man smiled at Stacey and gave her a free padded satin hanger before handing her mother the five pence change. The hanger was nearly as beautiful as the dress. Her mother had given her the Christmas dress early on the understanding that she never tell her father how much it had cost. The plum velvet was as smooth as a mouse, and she couldn't wait to show it off.

She daydreamed about her cousin and wished he were coming to the party. She imagined dancing with him, a slow dance. Maybe she'd kick off her shoes and they would spin out of the community centre and across the grass and over to Trewin's Wood, and she'd show him the Spy Club camp and its secret relics in the biscuit tin, and he might kiss her and they could get married. Cousins can . . . as long as they don't have babies.

Her mother picked up an egg in each hand and rolled them across the marble slab. Their cracking shells sounded like rice in a drum.

* * * * *

As the swarming rush of pain began to fade, Dorothy slumped back against the trunk of the oak. The moon reflected in the cracked Barbola mirror that still hung from its nail on the tree. She reached up and took the mirror down and studied her reflection in the glass. Her face was bright with sweat and red from exertion. When her waters broke late that afternoon, she had come straight to the camp. She didn't know why, but it seemed the only place she could go. It had still been light back then and the calls of roosting gulls and crows accompanied her first contraction, the birds' bodies black and white in the bare branches above her. That was two hours ago. She wrapped the crocheted bedspread tightly around her as the pain began to swarm again. She dropped the mirror as Lilly pushed her way through the narrow entrance to the camp. The glass cracked in three clean pieces.

"Oh Dorothy! Oh my God!" Lilly scrambled across to Dorothy's side and cradled her friend in her arms. "You can't do this! You can't have a baby here!"

Dorothy shook her head. "It's too late, Lilly. They're every two minutes. The book said it'll be here soon." Her face contorted as the pain drove her into the ground, her heels digging narrow furrows in the dirt. "You've got to help me, Lilly," she said. "It's got to be you."

"I don't know what to do! What do I do?"

"Think of the rabbits, Lilly. It's got to be like your Dad's rabbits." Dorothy picked up the checked towel and rammed it in her mouth as the scream flared in her chest.

Lilly took the flashlight and hung it from the nail that had housed the mirror. The funnel of light fell across Dorothy's legs, leaving her face in darkness. Lilly crouched down and gently pulled back the bedspread.

"Its head! I can see its head. Oh Dorothy, I've got to go and get someone!"

Dorothy ripped the towel from her mouth. "Stay the fuck where you are! I need you, Lilly." She sank back down into the dirt.

"I don't know when you need to push or anything!" Dorothy raised her legs and groaned, a sound that seemed to come from the ground and the tree and Dorothy all at the same time. " Oh my God," Lilly said. "Push, Dorothy! Push!"

Dorothy bore down into the dirt and threw her head back. Now that the oak had shed its leaves, she could see the first sparkle of stars through the criss-cross of its bare branches. She could feel the pain begin to rise again, but this time it was accompanied by a terrible heaviness that moved down her body like anaesthesia. The pain gripped her—mind and body—and there was nothing to do but ride through it.

She braced herself against the tree trunk and clawed at the birch branches Tot and Stacey had woven in and out of the bushes just six months earlier. They felt smooth and solid within her grip.

This time the contraction lasted longer, and she was seized with a burning need to push the child out of her body. If she could push it away, it would end. She braced again and screamed. Her cries seemed to weave their way up through the tree, across the branches, and spiral out towards the stars. The birds above her woke and flew, a wave of dark and light across the sky.

Lilly sat sobbing between Dorothy's knees. "It's a boy, Dorothy. It's a little boy. But I've got to cut the cord. We don't have anything!"

Dorothy shuddered and then pointed to the shortbread tin behind the tree. "The relics, Lilly. There's a knife and some string in the relic tin."

Lilly prized open the lid and pulled out the penknife and string. She cut two lengths of twine and tied off the cord tightly. She picked up the knife and tested it on the pad of her finger.

"Not yet," said Dorothy. "Give him to me."

The baby, who was streaked with blood and mud, took two or three gulps and then split the air with his first cry. Lilly wiped his mouth and nostrils with the hem of her skirt and handed him to Dorothy. She placed him on her breast, her actions directed by an ancient knowledge centuries older than her own.

"Dorothy, we've got to get you both to hospital. Just in case."

She kissed the baby on the forehead and shook her head. "No, Lilly. I need you to do something for me." She wrapped the child in the battenburg-checked towel and handed him to Lilly. "Put him somewhere where he'll be found."

"Where?"

Dorothy sat up against the trunk of the oak tree. "Put him in the community centre. They'll find him there."

"What about you?"

"I'll be all right." She picked up the crochet bedspread and folded it in half, then handed it to Lilly. "Wrap him in that. He mustn't get cold."

Lilly took the baby and reached into her pocket to retrieve Seamus's feather. She slipped it deep inside the folds of the rainbow-coloured bedspread.

* * * * *

Elaine Thompson lugged the large but light box of paper carnations out from the boot of the Rapier. The daylight had faded and a net of bright stars spread out across the sky above the Community Centre. There was no moon, but security lights illuminated the car park, washing the kids' playground with gaudy swipes of yellow and blue. The box was too big for her to carry, so she dropped it on the ground and pushed it with her foot across the tarmac into the lobby of the Bishop's Croft Community Centre.

Inside, the O'Flannerys were already setting up the bar. Mrs. O'Flannery was busy polishing glasses, and her husband busy drinking beer. A string of red and green fairy lights twisted in and out of the pump tags that hung over the bar. Mrs. O'Flannery secured one loose end with a piece of Sellotape, sticking it securely behind the plastic deer on the Babycham display. Mr. O'Flannery, with the air of a blessed man, stuck an empty pint glass below the Heineken tap and pulled on the pump. His wife slapped his hand and took the glass.

"Sean O'Flannery! It's ten-to-seven and that's three pints you've had already. It's all evening we've got in front of us, you know!" She rinsed the glass under the tap, snapped open the ring pull on a can of ginger ale, and handed it to him. She looked up and saw Elaine nudging the box through the open foyer doors. "Ah, Sean, here she is! Our very own interior decorator!" She bustled out from behind the bar and picked up the box in her ample arms. "Where do you want it, dear?"

Elaine pointed to the long bank of tables set in front of the life-size nativity display on the stage. "It'll be fine over there. Thank you, Veronica."

Mrs. O'Flannery carried the box across to the stage and dropped it on the middle table. "Now," she said, "what can I do to help?"

"Oh, really, you've done enough. I can take it from here."

"You know best, dear. And how's your two lovely girls today? All excited about the party?" Mrs. O'Flannery opened the box and began to unpack pink and red paper carnations, dumping them at rough intervals along the empty table. Elaine smiled and followed behind her, grouping them in threes on green card leaves she pulled from her pockets. "They're fine," she said. "Although I must admit, Dorothy pulled her usual disappearing act as soon as there was a sniff of work to be done."

"Just like my Lilly. I swear that girl has a work sensor in her brain! Oh, speak of the devil—"

Lilly struggled in through the fire doors with a large cardboard box.

"You're cutting it fine, young lady! Here we are, just ten minutes to go and no Perry glasses!"

Lilly nudged backwards through the kitchen swing doors, the heavy box cradled in front of her.

"Where are your brothers?" Mrs. Flannery asked.

Elaine placed the last of the card leaves on the table. "Lilly," she said. "Have you seen Dorothy?"

Lilly reappeared, shaking her head. "Michael and Seamus are on their way. I've got to go and change." She headed out for the fire doors.

"Remember, Lilly. Cleavage!" Mrs. O'Flannery turned back to Elaine. "But . . . it must be hard on your girls. Christmas, I mean. What with . . . what with their father gone. How long's it been now, dear? No word?"

"I got a letter last week. And fifteen pounds towards the girls' Christmas presents." She leant against the table and marvelled at how things could change in so short a time. Donald had been gone for six months. Stanley Close had rallied in his absence. Her front door step had become an altar to the deserted. It would magically fill with Kilner jars of stew, fruit pies, and bags of vegetables. The day before Guy Fawkes, a huge box of fireworks appeared, complete with matches and three pairs of knitted mittens.

And December had been humbling. The Stanley Close women had mobilised their husbands. They arrived with battered boxes of tools with which to fix her guttering, her stuck windows, the wonky bookcase over the piano. One day, she had awoken early to find Mr. Wright bent under the bonnet of her car. She never found out what he'd done, but after that the car had started without fail every morning. The red steps were also a source of information. Booklets on claiming child allowance appeared. Forms for social security. Applications for free school milk.

In the beginning, she had waited until it was dark before she opened the front door to pull everything inside into the hallway. Not any more. She merely filled the freezer and read the incomprehensible government forms late into the night.

And now he wanted to come back.

Mrs. O'Flannery put a plump arm around her shoulders. "Are you alright, dear? Me and my mouth. I shouldn't have mentioned the bastard."

"It's okay . . . you've all been so kind, and I don't deserve it."

"Leaving two kiddies like that. I'd break his bloody legs if I ever saw him again."

She squeezed the Irish woman's hand. "No need, Veronica. I think it was for the best. He wasn't happy and . . . looking back, I don't really blame him."

"Happy? HAPPY? Who said they've any right to bloody 'happy'? If they get three meals a day and sex on Fridays, they should be bloody delirious!"

"Excuse me, ladies. Where do you want these?" Mrs. Damson stood behind them holding a tray of deviled eggs and a bowl of salad. "Oh, and can we get into the kitchen? Gerald said he rinsed this salad, but I'd like to give it another going over."

"Leave those eggs here with Elaine. And yes, the kitchen's open," said Mrs. O'Flannery. "I had to stick the ice in the freezer. Can't bear the thought of vodka and orange with slushy ice!" She took the bowl of salad and shepherded Mrs. Damson towards the kitchen. She turned back to Elaine and pointed towards the foyer. "We better hurry up. It looks like the party's about to start."

The foyer was filling with neighbours hanging up coats and scarves. They brought in boxes and trays of snacks, pastries and fancy-cut sandwiches, and gossiped and laughed as they set them out between the paper carnations. Dips were sampled and praised, prawn *vol-au-vents* and slices of haslet piled onto paper plates, and the bar was three deep with orders for pints of beer and eggnog. Jimmy Deepens, splendid in a white suit, set up his turntables on the stage between the manger and the myrrh-bearing wise man. After a rather embarrassed "one-two, one-two" sound check, Michael Jackson opened the party with "Frosty the Snowman," and the residents of Stanley Close took to the dance floor.

Elaine parked herself at an empty table by the stage thanking God she'd made it this far when Tot arrived with Mr. and Mrs. Wright and Stacey.

"Where's Dorothy?" she asked Tot.

Her daughter shrugged. "Dunno. I thought she was with you."

Elaine looked at her watch. It was only seven-thirty. "Maybe she's still at Chris's."

Tot shook her head. "They broke up. Isn't Stacey's dress brilliant! Can we go to Wembley market?"

"Can I get you a drink, Elaine?" Mr. Wright pulled out a chair for his wife and hugged his daughter.

"Yes, thank you. I'll have a white wine spritzer. No ice."

"Can I have a Coca-Cola," asked Tot, "with a pickled onion in it?"

"Me too!" said Stacey, and both girls headed off towards the dance floor.

"Kids!" said Mr. Wright, then weaved his way through the dancers towards the bar.

By eight o'clock Elaine had had several dances with Mr. Wright and Mr. O'Flannery, each time their wives applauding from the edge of the dance floor. She'd even had a slow waltz with Mr. Damson, who complained bitterly that he couldn't get the hang of disco music. But she was worried about Dorothy, and the music and dancing had given her a headache. So she dug out her jacket from beneath the pile in the foyer and walked out into the car park to sip her wine on the low brick wall that bounded the perimeter of the Community Centre.

Outside, the net of stars had disappeared, but a huge moon shone through the red clouds above Trewin's Wood. It was snowing. Large dry flakes coated the pavement, the wind whipping miniature drifts into the gutters and along the wall by the side of the community centre. She left her wine glass on the low wall and ran back inside.

"Everyone! Everyone!" she shouted. "It's going to be a white Christmas!"

The partygoers emptied out into the car park to watch the first Christmas snow for four years. All except Seamus O'Flannery, who was playing silently in the Community Centre kitchen.

* * * * *

Seamus didn't like parties. There were too many people to become lost in, and he preferred the company of his sister and brother. But Lilly wasn't at the party. She'd disappeared to look for his trousers and never came back. And he didn't like his party jacket. The material was hairy and it was too tight across his stomach. His legs were cold and blotchy; Michael hadn't been able to find his trousers either and had given him a pair of football shorts to wear.

He knew his brother loved him, but didn't want to play with him. Instead, Michael sat with Mr. Deepens choosing records. Mr. Deepens had shouted at Seamus because he had run his finger along the smooth grooves on the records to feel where the music lived.

There were too many words out there in the main hall. All those people with so many words and there he was, with more words, better words, but no voice to say them with. It was quiet in the kitchen. The other people's words were still there, but they were muffled, and if he put his ear to the floor, he could feel the cold thump of the music through the tiles.

Cold outside. Warm in here. In this box where the glasses and bambies live, there's a rainbow blanket. Blankets don't live in boxes in kitchens. They live in the airing cupboard and on my bed.

He pulled out a yellow-tinged mixing bowl from the cupboard next to the box of Perry glasses and placed it on his head. It covered his eyes and through the glass, everything looked smoky. The white paintwork was now ice cream, the curtains over the sink the colour of winter meadow grass. He lay down on the tile floor and peered back at the box, the blanket now an orange-hued rainbow.

This box has got a rainbow in it and there's something in the rainbow. Something pink like a rabbit or a slipper.

He tugged the blanket. It was heavy and wrapped around something. A bambi? He lifted the bundle from the box and put it gently on the floor. He picked up a corner of the blanket between his thumb and finger and a small yellow-pink fist shook at him. He took the bowl off his head, then opened out the blanket. A baby kicked at the air. Its body was streaked with dried blood and mud and there were blades of grass in its red hair. Seamus touched the small fist with his finger. It gripped like a hug.

> The baby Jesus is in the kitchen. Jesus is in the kitchen! . . . careful. Mustn't drop Jesus like a bad man, or a king, or an emperor. Be a wise man. Carry the baby to the cradle. Carry Jesus to his Mummy, to the quiet lady in blue, to the man with the chipped beard. Put Jesus in the cradle. Tuck the blanket in the manger. Tuck him in like the baby in the rabbit skin.

* * * * *

Tot had only seen snow once when she was five. Her father had come home late one night and woken her up. He had carried her outside and shown her the back garden under six inches of glorious snow. She had buried her hands in it and tasted a mouthful before her mother arrived and whisked her back to bed. It had all disappeared by the following afternoon in a wave of rain.

Tonight, outside with the grownups from Stanley Close, she hoped the snow would stay. It made everyone quiet. Everyone looking up into the sky, tasting the flakes, gathering up tiny handfuls too dry to form into snowballs.

"Well, I don't know about you lot," said Mr. O'Flannery, "but my pint's going flat in there!" They all laughed and hurried back into the warmth of the community centre. Jimmy Deepens loaded another single on the record player, the dance floor filled, and the hungry grazed over the banquet table in search of the last *vol-au-vent*, a handful of crisp crumbs from the Tupperware bowls.

Tot sat next to her mother at the table by the stage. She was tired, and if she could, she would have slept. But this was a special night, and she intended to stay up as late as she could. She climbed up on the stage and looked at Mary, who was taller than she was and had a long roman nose. They should have given her a lovely nose, she thought. Joseph had one arm around Mary and looked down at the baby Jesus with a wondrous smile on his plaster face. His beard was chipped and missing a piece the size of a brazil nut. They were all a bit grubby. Even baby Jesus was grubby. Tot licked her finger and rubbed at a streak of brown on his leg. The red-headed Jesus wailed like a screech owl, and Tot fell off the stage. Their screams filled the air and drowned out Mr. Deepens's second airing of "Frosty the Snowman."

* * * * *

Elaine picked up the baby and held it underneath her jacket. It was warm, and she could feel it wriggle a little against her chest. Mrs. O'Flannery poked around in the manger for clues. All she found were three spice jars: cinnamon, cloves, and turmeric, nestled in the multi-coloured bedspread . . . and a feather. She stood the spices on the stage.

"Poor little mite," she said. "How's he doing?"

Elaine pulled down her jacket zipper and the baby's squeezed angry face looked out. He wailed and banged her chest with his fist. She laughed. "I think he's doing just fine. But where the hell's the ambulance? You okay, Tot?" Tot nodded. She had been brought another Coca-Cola and pickled onion and seemed none the worse for her fall.

Everyone milled around the hall. It seemed somehow irreverent to eat the last crackers or refill glasses until the baby had been taken care of.

Mr. Wright called from the foyer. "There're some lights coming. I think it's them."

Elaine heard the centre doors open and then clang shut. It wasn't the ambulance men. Two figures walked through the foyer and then stopped inside the double doors of the hall. Dorothy was silent and blue with cold. She was wearing her jeans and a jumper and her hair was a mess of soil and twigs. Lilly had her arm around her shoulder as if she was holding her up. Lilly whispered to Dorothy and the pair of them slowly walked up the middle of the dance floor, the staring sea of neighbours parting as the two girls came towards her.

Elaine could hear sirens.

Being an auntie is hard. There's babysitting and having to buy good presents at Christmas AND birthdays. And aunties have to knit things.

Knitting's hard too. You have to hold the needles and wind the wool around your fingers and then go in the front of the loop AND in the back if you want to do nobbly patterns. Then there's making things bigger and smaller and not dropping stitches. It's harder than Geography.

I'm knitting a scarf. It should be a matinée jacket or bootees, but I can only do squares and he's not. Square, I mean. So I'm just doing a skinny rectangle and not stopping. A scarf for baby Christian Donald Trampus Thompson. Dorothy let me choose one name.

Dad sent me a snow globe in the post. Inside is a silver unicorn standing on a rock and underneath, it says "Made in England." If you rub a unicorn's horn, your wishes come true.

But that would mean letting all the water out and anyway, aunties don't believe in wishes. They've got too much knitting to do.